M. Xavier

The Solitary of Juan Fernandez

Outlook

M. Xavier

The Solitary of Juan Fernandez

1. Auflage | ISBN: 978-3-73262-102-6

Erscheinungsort: Frankfurt am Main, Deutschland

Erscheinungsjahr: 2018

Outlook Verlag GmbH, Frankfurt.

THE SOLITARY OF JUAN FERNANDEZ;

OR, THE REAL ROBINSON CRUSOE

BY THE AUTHOR OF PICCIOLA.

TRANSLATED FROM THE FRENCH BY ANNE T. WILBUR.

MDCCCLI.

CONTENTS.

THE SOLITARY OF JUAN FERNANDEZ, OR THE REAL ROBINSON CRUSOE.

CHAPTER I.

The Royal Salmon.—Pretty Kitty.—Captain Stradling.—William Dampier. —Reveries and Caprices of Miss Catherine.

About the commencement of the last century, the little town of St. Andrew, the capital of the county of Fife, in Scotland, celebrated then for its University, was not less so for its Inn, the Royal Salmon, which, built in 1681 by a certain Andrew Felton, had descended as an inheritance to his only daughter, Catherine.

This young lady, known throughout the neighborhood under the name of pretty Kitty, had contributed not a little, by her personal charms, to the success and popularity of the inn. In her early youth, she had been a lively and piquant brunette, with black, glossy hair, combed over a smooth and prominent forehead, and dark, brilliant eyes, a style of beauty much in vogue at that period. Though tall and slender in stature, she was, as our ancestors would have said, sufficiently *en bon point.* In fine, Kitty merited her surname, and more than one laird in the neighborhood, more than one great nobleman even,—thanks to the familiarity which reigned among the different classes in Scotland,—had figured occasionally among her customers, caring as little what people might say as did the brave Duke of Argyle, whom Walter Scott has shown as conversing familiarly with his snuff merchant.

At present Catherine Felton is in her second youth. By a process common enough, but which at first appears contradictory, her attractions have diminished as they developed; her waist has grown thicker, the roses on her cheek assumed a deeper vermilion, her voice has acquired the rough and hoarse tone of her most faithful customers; the slender young girl is transformed into a virago. Fortunately for her, at the commencement of the eighteenth century, and especially in Scotland, reputations did not vanish as readily as in our days. Notwithstanding her increasing size and coarser voice, Catherine still remained pretty Kitty, especially in the eyes of those to whom she gave the largest credit.

Besides, if from year to year her beauty waned, a circumstance which might tend to diminish the attractions of her establishment, like a prudent woman she took care that her stock of ale and usquebaugh should also from year to year improve in quality, to preserve the equilibrium.

Undoubtedly the visits of lairds and great noblemen at her bar were less frequent than formerly, but all the trades-people in town, all the sailors in port, from the Gulf of Tay to the Gulf of Forth, still patronized the pretty landlady.

Meanwhile Catherine was not yet married. The gossips of the town were surprised, because she was rich and suitors were plenty; they fluttered around her constantly in great numbers, especially when somewhat exhilarated with wine. When their gallantry became obtrusive, Kitty was careful not to grow angry; she would smile, and lift up her white hand, tolerably heavy, till the offenders came to order. Catherine possessed in the highest degree the art of restraining without discouraging them, and always so as to forward the interests of her establishment.

To maintain the discipline of the tavern, nevertheless, the presence of a man was desirable; she understood this. Besides, the condition of an old maid did not seem to her at all inviting, and she did not care to wait the epoch of a third youth, before making a choice. But what would the unsuccessful candidates say? Would not this decision be at the risk of kindling a civil war, of provoking perhaps a general desertion? Then, too, accustomed as she was to command, the idea of giving herself a master alarmed her.

She was vacillating amid all these perplexities, when a certain sailor, with cold and reserved manners, whose face bore the mark of a deep sabre cut, and who had for some time past, frequented her inn with great assiduity, without ever having addressed to her a single word, took her aside one fine morning and said:

'Listen to me, Kate, and do not reply hastily. I came here, not like many others, attracted by your beautiful eyes, but because I wished to obtain recruits for an approaching voyage which I expected to undertake at my own risk and peril. I do not know how it has happened, but I now think less about sailing; I seem to be stumbling over roots. Right or wrong, I imagine that a good little wife, who will fill my glass while I am tranquilly smoking my pipe before a blazing fire, may have as many charms as the best brig in which one may sometimes perish with hunger and thirst. Right or wrong, I imagine to myself again that the prattle of two or three little monkeys around me, may be as agreeable as the sound of the wind howling through the masts, or of Spanish balls whistling about one's ears. All this, Kate, signifies that I mean to marry; and who do you suppose has put this pretty whim into my head? who, but yourself?'

Catherine uttered an exclamation of surprise, perfectly sincere, for if she had expected a declaration, it was certainly not from this quarter.

'Do not reply to me yet,' hastily resumed the sailor; 'he who pronounces his decree before he has heard the pleader and maturely reflected on the case, is a poor judge. To continue then. You are no longer a child, Kate, and I am no longer a young man; you are approaching thirty—'

At these words the pretty Kitty made a gesture of surprise and of denial.

'Do not reply to me!' repeated the pitiless sailor. 'You are thirty! I have already passed another barrier, but not long since. We are of suitable age for each other. The man should always have traversed the road before his companion. You are active and genteel; that does very well for women. You have always been an honest girl, that is better still. As for me, my skin is not so white as yours, but it is the fault of a tropic sun. It is possible that I may be a little disfigured by the scar on my cheek; but of this scar I am proud; I had the honor of receiving it, while boarding a vessel, from the hand of the celebrated Jean Bart, who, after having on that occasion lost a fine opportunity of being honorably killed, has just suffered himself to die of a stupid pleurisy; but it is not of him but of myself that we are now to speak. After having fought with Jean Bart, I have made a voyage with our not less celebrated William Dampier, whom I may dare call my friend. You may therefore understand, Kate, that if you have the reputation of an honest girl, I have that of a good sailor. The name of Captain Stradling is favorably known upon two oceans, and it will be to your credit, if ever, with your arm linked in mine, we walk as man and wife, through any port of England or Scotland. I have said. Now, look, reflect; if my proposition suits you, I will settle for life on *terra firma*, and bid adieu to the sea; if not, I resume my projected expedition, and it will be to you, Kate, that I shall say adieu.'

Catherine opened her mouth to thank him, as was suitable, for his good intentions.

'Do not reply to me!' interrupted he again; 'in three days I will come to receive your decision.'

And he went out, leaving her amazed at having listened to so long a speech from one, who until then, seated motionless in a distant corner of the room, had always appeared to her the most rigid and silent ofseamen.

That very day Catherine has come to a decision concerning the captain; she thinks him ugly and disagreeable, coarse and ignorant; he has dared to tell her that she is thirty years old, and she will hardly be so at St. Valentine's Day, which is six weeks ahead, at least. Besides the scar which he has received from the celebrated Jean Bart, his countenance has no beauty to boast of: his face is long and pale, his temples are furrowed with wrinkles, and his lips thick and heavy; his eyebrows, at the top of his forehead, seem to be lost in his hair; his eyes are not mates, his nose is one-sided; his form is perhaps still worse; he walks after the fashion of a duck. Fie! can such a man be a suitable match for the rich landlady of the Royal Salmon, for the beautiful Kitty; for her who, among so many admirers and lovers, has had but the difficulty of a choice?

The next day towards nightfall, Catherine, seated in her bar, in the large leathern arm-chair which served as her throne, with dreamy and downcast brow, and chin resting on her hand, was still thinking of Captain Stradling, but her ideas had assumed a different aspect from those of the evening before.

She was saying to herself: 'If he has thick and heavy lips, it is because he is an Englishman; if he walks like a duck, it is because he is a sailor; if he has taken me to be thirty years old, that proves simply that he is a good physiognomist, and I shall have one painful avowal the less to make after marriage. As for his scar, he has a thousand reasons to be proud of it, and, upon close examination, it is not unbecoming. It would be very difficult for me to choose a husband, on account of the discontented suitors who will be left in the lurch; but I will relinquish my business, and that will put an end to all inconvenience. He is rich, so much for the profit; he is a captain, so much for the honor. Come, come, Mistress Stradling will have no reason to complain!'

At this moment, Catherine Felton could meditate quite at her ease, without fear of being noticed; for the tobacco smoke, three times as dense and abundant as usual, enveloped her in an almost opaque cloud. There was this evening a grand *fête* at the tavern of the Royal Salmon. The concourse of customers was immense, and this time, it was neither the beauty of the hostess, nor the quality of the liquors which had attracted them thither.

The serving-men and lasses were going from table to table, multiplying themselves to pour out, not only the golden waves of strong beer and usquebaugh, but the purple waves of claret and port; all faces were smiling, all eyes sparkling, and in the midst of the huzzas and *vivas*, was heard, with triple applause, the name of William Dampier.

This celebrated man, now a corsair, now a skilful seaman, who had just discovered so many unknown straits and shores, who had just made the tour of the world twice, in an age when the tour of the world did not pass, as at present, for a trifling matter; who had published, upon his return, a narrative full of novel facts and observations; this pitiless and intelligent pirate, who studied the coasts of Peru while he pillaged the cities along its shores, and meditated, in the midst of tempests, his learned theory of winds and tides,

William Dampier, had landed, this very day at the little port of St. Andrew.

At the intelligence of his arrival, the whole maritime population of the coast was in commotion; the society of the *Old Pilots*, with that of the *Sea Dogs*, had sent to him deputations, headed by the principal ship-owners in the town. Captain Stradling had not failed to be among them, happy at the opportunity of once more meeting and embracing his former friend. Speeches were made, as if to welcome an admiral, speeches in which were passed in review all his noble qualities and the great services rendered by him to the marine interest. To these Dampier replied with simplicity and conciseness, saying to the orators:

'Gentlemen and dear comrades, you must be hoarse, let us drink!'

This first trait of eccentricity could not fail to enlist universal applause.

Commissioned by him to lead the column, Stradling could not do otherwise than to take the road to the Royal Salmon. It was on this occasion that he appeared there before the expiration of the three days: but he had not addressed a word to Catherine, scarcely turned his eyes towards her. Nevertheless the circumstances were favorable to his suit.

Then a millionaire, William Dampier had immediately declared his intentions to treat at his own expense the whole company and even the whole town, if the town would do him the honor to drink with him. Catherine at once took him into favor. When she heard him praise his friend and companion, the brave Captain Stradling, she felt for the latter, not an emotion of tenderness, but a sentiment of respect and even of good-will. Dampier, excited by his audience, did not fail, like other conquerors by land and sea, to recount some of his great deeds. Among others, he recapitulated a certain affair in which he and his friend Stradling had captured a Spanish galleon, laden with piastres. From this moment the beautiful Kitty became more thoughtful, and began to see that the scar was becoming to the face of this good captain. After drinking, when Dampier, still escorted by his *fidus Achates*, came to settle his account with the hostess, he chucked her familiarly under the chin, as was his custom with landladies in the four quarters of the globe. From any one else, the proud Catherine would not have suffered such a liberty; to this, she replied only by a graceful reverence, and, while the hero and paymaster of the *fête* shook a rouleau of gold upon her counter, she said, hastily bending towards Stradling:

'To-morrow!' accompanying this word with an expressive look and her most gracious smile.

The enamored Stradling, always impassible, contented himself with replying:

'It is well!'

The day following, the third, the important day, that which Catherine already regarded as her day of betrothal, early in the morning, she dressed herself in her best attire, not doubting the impatience of the captain. Before noon, the latter entered the inn and went directly up to the landlady.

She received him carelessly and coldly; she was nervous, she had not had time for reflection; she did not know what the captain wished; if he would let her alone for the present, by and by she would consider.

'Boy! a new pipe and some ale!' exclaimed Stradling, addressing a waiter.

And, perfectly calm in appearance, he sauntered to his accustomed place at the farther end of the bar-room. However, before leaving the Royal Salmon, approaching Catherine, he said:

'Yesterday, by your voice and gesture you said, or almost said, yes; we sailors know the signals; to-day it is no, or almost no. Very well, I will wait; but reflect, my beauty, we are neither of us young enough to lose our time in this foolish game.'

But what had thus unexpectedly changed, from white to black, the good intentions of Catherine in the captain's behalf? The presence of a young boy whom she had not seen for many years, and towards whom she had, until then, felt only a kindly indifference.

CHAPTER II.

Alexander Selkirk.—The College.—First Love.—Eight Years of Absence. —Maritime Combats.—Return and Departure.—The Swordfish.

Alexander Selkirk,—the name of the principal personage in this narrative,—was born at Largo, in the county of Fife, not far from St. Andrew. Entered as a pupil in the university of the town, he at first distinguished himself by his aptitude and his intelligence, until the day when, hearing of the beauty of the landlady of the Royal Salmon, he was seized with an irresistible desire to see her: he saw her, and became violently enamored. It was one of those youthful passions, springing rather from the effervescence of the age, than from the merit of the object; one of those sudden ebullitions to which the young recluses of science are sometimes subject, from a prolonged compression of the natural and affectionate sentiments.

From this moment, all the words in the Greek and Latin dictionaries, all the principles of natural philosophy, mathematics and history, suddenly taken by storm, whirled confusedly and pell-mell in the head of Selkirk, like the elements of the world in chaos, before the day of creation.

His professors had predicted that at the annual exhibition he would obtain six great prizes; he obtained not even a premium.

As a punishment, he was required to remain within the college grounds during the vacation. But its gates were not strong enough, nor its walls high enough to detain him.

Condemned, for the crime of desertion, to a classic imprisonment, he was shut up in a cellar; he escaped through the window; in a garret; he descended by the roof.

Then, pronounced incorrigible, he was expelled from the university.

He left it joyous and happy, escaped from the tutor commissioned to conduct him to his father, and at last wholly free, his own master, he took lodgings in a cabin, not far from the Royal Salmon, and thought himself monarch of the universe.

As soon as the doors of the inn were opened, he penetrated there with the earliest fogs of morning, with the first beams of day; in the evening he was the last to cross the threshold, after the extinction of the lights.

All day long, seated at a little table opposite the bar, between a pipe and a pewter pot, he watched the movements of Kitty, and followed her with admiring eyes.

Catherine was not slow to perceive this new passion; but she was accustomed to admiring eyes, and therefore paid but little heed to them. She was then at the age of twenty-two, in all the glory of her transient royalty; he, scarcely sixteen, was in her eyes a boy, a raw and awkward boy, like almost all the other students, and she contented herself with now and then bestowing a slight smile upon him, in common with her other customers.

But this mechanical smile, this half extinguished spark, did but increase the flame, by kindling in the young man's soul a ray of hope.

At this age, passion has not yet an oral language; it is in the heart, in the head especially, but not on the lips; one comprehends, experiences, dreams, writes of love in prose and verse, but does not talk of it. Selkirk had twenty times attempted to confess his affection to Catherine; he had as yet succeeded only in a few simple and hasty meteorological sentences, on the rain and fine weather. He therefore wrote.

Unfortunately, Catherine could not easily read writing; she applied to him to interpret his letter. This was a hard task for the poor boy, who, with a tremulous and hesitating voice, saw himself forced to stammer through all that burning phraseology which seemed to congeal under the breath of the reader.

The result however was that Catherine became his friend; she encouraged his confidence, and gave him good advice as an elder sister might have done. She even called him by the familiar name of Sandy, which was a good omen.

Meanwhile his scanty resources became exhausted; he had no longer means to pay for the pot of ale which he consumed daily. The idea of asking credit of his beloved, of opening with her an account, which he might never have means to pay, was revolting to him. On the other hand, the thought of returning home, and asking pardon of his father, was not less repugnant to his feelings. He was endowed with one of those haughty and imperious natures which recognize their faults, not to repair them, but to make of them a starting point, or even a pedestal.

He was rambling about the port, reflecting on his unfortunate situation, when he heard mention made of a ship ready to set sail at high tide, and which needed a reinforcement of cabin-boys and sailors. This was for him an inspiration; he did not hesitate, he hastened to engage. That very evening he had gained the open sea, beyond the Isle of May, and, with his eyes turned towards the Bay of St. Andrew, was attempting, in vain, to recognize among the lights which were yet burning in the city, the fortunate lantern which decorated the sacred door of the Royal Salmon.

At present, Alexander Selkirk is twenty-four years old. He has become a genuine sailor, and he loves his profession; the sea is now his beautiful Kitty. Besides, it is long since he has troubled himself about his heart. It is empty, even of friendship, for, among his numerous companions, the proud young man has not found one worthy of him. After having served two years in the merchant marine, he has entered the navy. Thanks to the war kindled in Europe for the Spanish succession, he has for a long time cruised with the brave Admiral Rooke along the coasts of France; with him, he has fought against the Danish in the Baltic Sea, and in 1702, in the capacity of a master pilot, figured honorably in the expedition against Cadiz, and in the affair of Vigo. Finally, under the command of Admiral Dilkes, he has just taken part in the destruction of a French fleet.

But all these expeditions, rather military than maritime, and circumscribed in the narrow circle of the seas of Europe, have not satisfied the vast desires of the ambitious sailor. He experiences an invincible thirst to apply his knowledge, to exercise his intelligence on a larger scale; he is impatient for a long voyage, a voyage of discovery.

The terrific hurricane of the twenty-seventh of November, 1703, which drove the waves of the Thames even into Westminster, Hall, and covered London almost entirely with the fragments of broken vessels, appeared to Selkirk a favorable occasion for asking his dismissal. He easily obtained it. So many sailors had just been thrown out of employment by the hurricane.

Once more, the undisciplined scholar found himself free and his own master! He profited by this to pay a visit to his birthplace in Scotland. His father was dead, but he had some business to regulate there.

On reaching Largo he learned the arrival of William Dampier at St. Andrew. He set sail for that port immediately.

'Ah!' said he on his way, 'if this brave captain should be about to undertake a voyage to the New World, and will let me accompany him, no matter in what capacity, all my wishes will be gratified. I thirst to see tattooed faces, other trees besides beeches, oaks and firs; other shores than those of the Baltic, Mediterranean and Atlantic. Who knows whether I may not aid him in the discovery of some new continent, some unknown island which shall bear my name!'

And, cradled by the wave in the frail canoe that bore him, he dreamed of government, perhaps of royalty, in one of those archipelagoes which he imagined to exist in the bosom of the distant Southern seas, long afterwards explored by Cook, Bougainville and Vancouver.

Once in port, he hastened to inquire for the dwelling occupied by Dampier. The latter was absent; he was in the harbor.

While awaiting his return, our young sailor thought of his old friend Catherine, his pretty black-eyed Kitty, and directed his steps towards the inn.

He found her already enthroned in her leathern arm-chair, her hair neatly braided, with two small curls on her temples; in a toilette which the early hour of the morning did not seem to authorize; but it was the famous third day, and she was awaiting Stradling.

On seeing Selkirk enter, she exclaimed to the boy, pointing to the newly-arrived: 'A pot of ale!'

'No,' cried the young man smiling; 'the ale which I once drank here was for me a philter full of bitterness; a glass of whiskey, if you please,—' and, pointing to the little table opposite the bar at which he was formerly accustomed to place himself, he said:

'Serve me there; I will return to my old habits.'

Catherine looked at him with astonishment.

'Does not pretty Kate recognize me?' said he in a caressing tone, approaching her.

'How! Is it possible! is it you, indeed, Sandy?'

'Yes, Alexander Selkirk, formerly a fugitive from the University of St. Andrew; recently a master pilot in the royal marine; now, as ever, your very humble servant.'

And they shook hands, and examined each other closely, but the impression on both sides was far from being the same.

Catherine finds Selkirk much changed, but for the better; time and navigation have been favorable to him. He is no longer the raw student with embarrassed air, awkward manner, bony frame and dilapidated costume; but a stout young man, with a broad chest, active and graceful form; though his features are decidedly Scotch, they are handsome; his eyes, less brilliant than formerly, are animated with a more attractive thoughtfulness, and the naval uniform, which he still wears, sets off his person to advantage.

On his part, Selkirk finds Catherine also much changed; the rosy complexion, the soft voice, the youthful look, the twenty-two years, all are gone. Her form has assumed a superabundant amplitude.

They drop each other's hands and utter a sigh; he, of regret; she, of surprise.

Both close their eyes, at the same time; she, with the fear of gazing too earnestly; he, to recall the being of his imagination.

However this may be, she is not yet a woman to be despised by a sailor. He therefore prolongs his visit: they come to interrogations, to confidences.

Catherine acquaints him with the situation of her little business affairs; her fortune is improving; she gives him an estimate of it in round numbers, as well as of the suitors she has rejected; but she does not mention Captain Stradling, whose arrival she yet fears every moment.

Selkirk relates to her his campaigns, his combats against the French, against the Danish, the victorious attack of the English ships against the great boom of Vigo; but, when she asks him what motive has brought him back to St. Andrew, he replies boldly that he came to see her and no one else, and says not a word of Captain Dampier, whom he is even now impatient to meet.

At last the old friends say adieu.

Then the gallant sailor, with an apparent effort, goes away, not forgetting, however, to drink his glass of whiskey.

And this is the reason why, on the third day, Catherine has the vapors; this is the reason why, notwithstanding her soft words of the evening before and her grand morning toilette, she receives so coldly the scarred adversary of the celebrated Jean Bart.

During the whole of the week following, Stradling, Dampier and Selkirk, did not fail to meet at the Royal Salmon. Selkirk came to see Dampier; Dampier came to see Stradling; Stradling came to see Catherine Felton.

The latter thought the young man already knew the two others, that he had sailed with them, and was not surprised at their intimacy.

Sometimes Selkirk, leaving his companions in the midst of their bottles and glasses, would describe a tangent towards the counter, and come to converse with the pretty hostess. He no longer felt love for her, and notwithstanding this, perhaps for this very reason, he now talked eloquently.

Kitty blushed, was embarrassed, and poor Captain Stradling, listening with all his ears to the narratives of his illustrious friend William Dampier, or pre-occupied with his pipe, lost in its cloud, saw nothing,—or seemed to see nothing.

Nevertheless one evening, he went, in his turn, to lean on the counter:

'Kate,' said he, 'when is our marriage to take place?'

'Are you thinking of that still?' replied she, with an air of levity which would once have became her better; 'I hoped this fancy had passed out of your head.'

'I may then set out on my voyage, Kate?'

'Why not? We will talk of our plans on your return.'

'But I am going to make the tour of the world, as well as my friend Dampier. Kate, it is the affair of three years!'

'So much the better! it will give us both time for reflection.'

'It is well!' replied the phlegmatic Englishman, and nothing on his polar face betokened an afterthought.

The doors closed, the lights extinguished, Catherine retired to rest the happiest woman in the world. She said to herself: 'Alexander loves me, and has loved me for eight years! he deserves to be rewarded. He has less money than the other, it is a misfortune; but he has more youth and grace, that balances it. As to rank, a master pilot of twenty-four is as far advanced as a captain of forty. Between Selkirk and myself, if the wealth is on my side, on his will be gratitude and little attentions. At all events, I prefer a young husband who will whisper words of love in my ear, to amusing myself by pouring out drink for my lord and master, while he smokes his pipe, with his feet on the brands. Was it not thus that icicle, dressed in blue, called Stradling, talked to me of the pleasures of marriage? And what a name! But Mistress Selkirk!—that sounds well. In our Scotland, there is the county of Selkirk, the town of Selkirk; there is even a great nobleman of this name, who is something like minister to our Queen Anne, I believe. Who knows? we are perhaps of his family! As for walking about the port arm-in-arm with a captain, I am sure my very dear friends and neighbors would die with jealousy if I took, instead of this scarred captain, a young and handsome man. It is settled. I will marry Alexander; to-morrow I will myself announce it to him. I hope he will not die of joy!'

On the morrow she attired herself as on the day of Selkirk's return, in her beautiful dress of cloth and silk, with the two little curls upon her temples. She thus waited a great part of the day. At last, about four o'clock, Selkirk arrives in haste, his face beaming with joy, and a gleam of triumph in his eye.

'Has he then,' thought Catherine, 'a presentiment of the happiness in store for him?'

'Congratulate me, pretty Kitty,' said the young man, almost out of breath; 'I am appointed mate of the brig Swordfish, which I am to join at Dunbar.'

'How! you are going?'

'In an hour.'

'For a long time?'

'For three years at least. In a fortnight we set sail for the East Indies. It will be a great commercial voyage and a voyage of discovery. Unfortunately William Dampier does not accompany us; but he furnishes funds to the brave Captain Stradling.'

'Stradling!'

'Yes, it is he who has just engaged me, and with whom I am to sail. Our agreement is signed,—I am mate! I am going to explore the New World! Ah! I would not exchange my fate for that of a king. But time presses; adieu, Kitty, till I see you again!'

'Three years!' murmured Catherine.

And her curls grew straight beneath the cold perspiration that covered her forehead.

CHAPTER III.

The Tour of the World.—The Way to manufacture Negroes—California. —The Eldorado.—Revolt of Selkirk.—The Log-Book.—Degradation. —A Free Shore.

The Swordfish, well provisioned, even with guns and ammunition, left Dunbar one morning with a fresh breeze, sailed down the North Sea, passed Ireland, France and Spain, the Azores, Canaries, and Cape Verd Islands on the coast of Africa, and, after having stopped for a short time in the harbors of Guinea and Congo, doubled the Cape of Good Hope, amid the traditional tempest.

Entering the Indian Ocean, and passing through the Straits of Sunda, she touched at Borneo, and at Java, reached the Southern Sea by the Gulf of Siam, passed the Philippine Isles, then, through the vast regions of the Pacific Ocean, pursued the route which had been marked out by the exploring ship of William Dampier in 1686. Like that, the Swordfish remained a few days at the Island of St. Pierre, before launching into that immensity where, during nearly two months, wave only succeeded to wave; at last she reached the coasts of South America, and cast anchor in the Gulf ofCalifornia.

This gigantic voyage, which seemed as if it must have been attempted under the inspiration of science and with the hope of the most important discoveries, had been undertaken by Stradling with no object but of traffic and even of rapine. These had been the great ends of most of the bold enterprises which had preceded. The Spanish and Portuguese, in their discoveries of new continents, had thought less of glory than of riches; they had conquered the New World only to pillage it; the vanquished who escaped extermination, were forced to dig their native soil, not to render it more fruitful, but to procure from it, for the profit of the vanquisher, the gold it might contain. Among the European nations, those who had had no part in the conquest now sought to share the spoils. For this the least pretext of war or commerce sufficed.

Stradling availed himself of both these pretences; when he touched at the coasts of Guinea and Congo, it was to obtain negroes whom he expected to sell in America. At Borneo, the opportunity presented itself for an advantageous disposal of the greater part of his black merchandize; as he was a man of resources and not at all scrupulous, he soon found means to replace them.

In the Straits of Sunda, several barques, manned by negroes and Malays, had become entangled in the masses of seaweed which are every where floating on the surface of the wave; Stradling encountered them, made the rowers enter his ship, and obligingly took the barques in tow, to extricate them from their difficulty. But those who ascended the side of the Swordfish, descended only to be sold in their turn.

Although he had received an education superior to that of his companions, Selkirk shared in the prejudices of his times; he had therefore found nothing objectionable in seeing his captain exchange at Congo little mirrors, a few glass beads, half a dozen useless guns, and some gallons of brandy, for men still young and vigorous, torn from their country and their families. Their skin was of another color, their heads woolly; this was a profitable traffic, recognized by governments; but when he saw Stradling seize the property of others to refill his empty hold, he could not control his indignation and boldly expressed it:

'It is for their salvation,' replied the captain, without emotion; 'we will make Christians of them.'

On approaching the Vermilion Sea, a deep gulf which separates California from the American continent, and makes it almost an island, the Malays were rubbed with a mixture of tar and dragon's blood, dissolved in a caustic oil, to give to their olive skins a deeper shade, and their flat noses and silky hair making them pass for Yolof negroes, they were exchanged at Cape St. Lucas, along with the rest, for pearls and native productions.

Thc young mate thought this proceeding not less mean and dishonorable than the first; he made new observations.

'Nothing now remains to be done, captain,' said he, 'but to shave and besmear with tar the monkey you have just bought, and to include it among your new race of negroes.'

This time, the captain looked at him askance, and shrugged his shoulders without replying.

The storm was beginning to growl in the distance.

It was not without a secret object that, in his course through the Southern Sea, Stradling had first of all aimed at California.

He devoted an entire month to cruising along both shores of this almost island, and penetrating all the bays of the Vermilion Sea; he hoped to find there a passage to an unknown land, then predicted and coveted by all navigators. What was this land? The *Eldorado*!

Although I would hasten over these details of the voyage to arrive at the more important events of this history; now that the recent discovery of the immense mines of gold buried beneath the hills of California has aroused the entire world, that the name alone of *Sacramento* seems to fill with gold the mouth which pronounces it, there is a curious fact, perhaps entirely unknown, which I cannot pass over in silence.

After the middle of the sixteenth century, and long before the seventeenth, a vague rumor, a confused tradition, had located, in the neighborhood of the Vermilion Sea, a famed land, whose rivers rolled over gold, and whose mountains rested on golden foundations; the treasures of Mexico and Peru were nothing in comparison with those which were to be gathered there. An ingot of native gold was talked of, of a *pepite* or eighty pounds weight.

It was a grape from the promised land.

This marvellous country had been named, in advance, *Eldorado*.

Among the bold Argonauts of these two centuries, there was a contest as to who should first raise his flag over this new Colchis, defended, it was said, by the Apaches, a terrible, sanguinary and cannibal race, whom Cortez himself could not subdue. This land of gold some had located in New Biscay or New Mexico; others, in the pretended kingdoms of Sonora and Quivira; then, after several ineffectual attempts, the possibility of reaching it was denied; learned men, from the various academies of Europe, proved that the *Eldorado* was not a country, but a dream; on this subject the Old World laughed at the New; the Argonauts became discouraged, and during a century the subject was named only to be ridiculed.

And yet, in spite of sceptics and scoffers, the *Eldorado* existed. It existed where tradition had placed it, on the shores of this Vermilion Sea, now the Gulf of California. For once, popular opinion had the advantage over scientific dissertations and philosophic denials; there, where, according to the Dictionary of Alcedo, nothing had been discovered but mines of pewter! where Jacques Baegert had indeed acknowledged the presence of gold, but *in meagre veins*; where Raynal had named as curiosities only fishes and pearls, declaring, in California, *the sea richer than the land*; where in our own times M. Humboldt discovered nothing but cylindrical cacti, on a sandy soil, remained buried, as a deposit for future ages, this treasure of the world, which seemed to be waiting in order to leave its native soil, the moment of falling into the hands of a commercial and industrious people, that of the United States.

This *Eldorado*, Stradling sought in vain; he therefore decided to pursue his route along the coast of Mexico, now under the French flag, when he found an opportunity for traffic with the natives, colonists or savages; now under the English flag, when he wished to exercise his trade of corsair, an easy profession, for since the disaster of Vigo, the Spanish had abandoned their transatlantic possessions to themselves.

The Spanish soldiery of America then found themselves, in the presence of European adventurers, in that state of pusillanimous inferiority in which had been, at the period of the conquest, the subjects of the Incas and Montezuma before the soldiers of Cortez and Pizarro. The time was not already far passed, when a few bands of freebooters, from France, England and Holland, had well nigh wrested from his Majesty, the King of Spain and the Indies, the most extensive and wealthy of his twenty-two hereditary kingdoms.

Stradling was following in the footsteps of these freebooters.

Recently, two little cities on the coast had been put under contribution for the supplies of the Swordfish; there had been resistance, a threatened attack, a parley, and capitulation; in this affair, the young mate had nobly distinguished himself both as a combatant and a negotiator, and yet the captain had not deigned to give him a share in his distribution of compliments.

Selkirk felt an irritation the more lively that this shore life began to be irksome. Not that his conscience disturbed him any more than in the treatment of the blacks; he thought it as honorable to war with the Spaniards in the New World, as to be beaten by them in the Old; but he compared his present chief, Captain Stradling, with his former commander, the noble and brave Admiral Rooke; the parallel extended in his mind to his old companions in the royal navy, all so frank, so gay, so loyal,—among whom he had yet never found a friend,—and his new companions of to-day, recruited for the most part in the marshy lowlands of the merchant marine of Scotland; his thoughts became overshadowed, and his desires for independence, which dated from his college life, returned in full force.

As much as his duties permitted, he loved to isolate himself from all; when he could remain some time alone in his cabin, or gaze upon the sea from a retired corner of the deck and watch the ploughing of the vessel, then only he was happy.

As if to increase his uneasiness, Stradling became daily more severe and more exacting towards his chief officer; he imposed upon him rude labors foreign to his station. It seemed as if he were determined to drive him to desperation.

He succeeded.

Selkirk protested against such treatment, and recapitulated his subjects of complaint. The other paid no more attention than he would have done to the buzzing of a fly.

Irritated by this outrageous impassibility, the young man declared that there should no longer be any thing in common between them, and that, whatever fate might await him, he demanded to be set on shore.

Stradling touched his forehead:

'That is a good idea,' said he, and he turned away.

The next day, they reached the Isthmus of Panama; the persevering Selkirk returned to the charge: 'The moment is favorable for ridding yourself of me, and me of you,' said he to the captain; 'let the boat convey me to the shore; I will cross the Isthmus, reach the Gulf of Darien, the North Sea, and return to Scotland, even before the Swordfish!'

This time the honest corsair listened attentively, then shaking his head and winking his eye, with the smile of a hungry vampire, replied:

'You are then in great haste to be married, comrade.'

It was the first word he had addressed to him relative to Catherine during this long voyage, and this word Selkirk had not even understood.

They were about passing Panama: the vessel continuing her voyage, Selkirk interposed his authority, ordered the men to put about, take in sail and approach the shore.

This Stradling prohibited, uttered a formidable oath, and commanded the young man to bring the log-book. When it was brought, he made the following entry:

'To-day, Sept. 24th, 1704, Alexander Selkirk, mate of this vessel, having mutinied and attempted to desert to the enemy, we have deprived him of his title and his office; in case of obstinacy we shall hang him to the yard-arm.'

And he read the sentence to the offender.

From this day, the rebel saw himself compelled to serve in the Swordfish as a simple sailor, and his subordinates of yesterday, to-day his equals, indemnified themselves for the authority he had exercised over them, which did not cure him of that native contempt he had always felt for mankind.

A month passed away thus, during which the Swordfish several times touched the shores of Peru, now to renew her supplies of provisions and water, now to exchange with the Indians, nails, hatchets, knives, and necklaces of beads, for gold dust, furs, and garments trimmed with colored feathers.

During one of these pauses, Selkirk, left on the ship, accosted the captain once more. He knew that the remains of some bands of freebooters were colonized there, leading a peaceful and agricultural life; this fact was known to all. At Coquimbo in Chili, some English and Dutch pirates had formed a settlement of this kind, now in the full tide of prosperity. Selkirk, who, during an entire month, had not spoken to the captain, now demanded, in a voice which he attempted to render calm and almost supplicating, to be landed at Coquimbo, from which they were only a few days sail.

'You will not this time accuse me of wishing to desert to the enemy; they are the English, Scotch, Dutch, our countrymen and allies whom I wish to join! Do you still suspect me? Well, do not content yourself with setting me on shore; place me in the hands of the chief men of the settlement. Will that suit you?'

Stradling winked significantly; but this was all.

'Ah!' resumed the young man with increasing emotion, 'do not think to detain me longer on board, to crush me beneath this humiliation! I consented to serve under your orders as mate, and you have made me the lowest of your sailors; this you had no right to do.'

Stradling took his glass and directed it towards the shore, where his people were engaged in trafficking their beads and hardware.

Raising his head and folding his arms:

'Captain,' pursued Selkirk with vehemence, 'some day or other we shall return to England, where the laws protect all; there, I shall have the right of complaint, and Queen Anne loves to render justice; beware!'

Stradling, still spying, began to whistle *God save the Queen*; then he called his monkey and made it gambol before him.

'I will depart, I will free myself from your presence, and that of your worthy companions; I will do so at all events, do you understand!' exclaimed Selkirk exasperated, 'I will not endure your infamous treatment another week! If you refuse to consent to my demand, I will leave without your permission; were the vessel twenty miles from the land, and were I to perish twenty times on the way, I will attempt to swim ashore. Will you land me at Coquimbo, yes or no? Reply!'

By way of reply, Stradling ordered him to be confined in the hold.

Poor Selkirk! Ah! if pretty Kitty, if the beautiful landlady of the Royal Salmon could know all thou hast endured for her sake, how many tears would her fine eyes shed over thy fate! But who knows whether she will ever hear of thee? Who can tell whether any human being will learn the sufferings in reserve for thee?

Poor Selkirk! you who painted to yourself so smiling a picture of this grand voyage to America; who hoped to leave, like Dampier, your name to some strait, some newly discovered island; you who dreamed of scientific walks in vast prairies and under the arches of virgin forests, you have shared only in the career of a trafficker and a pirate; of this New World, full of marvellous sights, you have seen only the shore, the fringe of the mantle, the margin of this last work of God!

Poor Selkirk, must you then return to your cold and foggy Scotland, without having contemplated at your ease, beneath the brilliant sun of the tropics, one of those Edens overshadowed by the luxuriant verdure of palm-trees, bananas, mimosas and gigantic ferns? In your country, the bark of the trees is clad with lichens and mosses, and the parasite mistletoe suspends itself to the branches, more as a burden than as an ornament; here, numerous families of the orchis, with their singular forms, showy and variegated blossoms, climb along the knotty stems of the tall monarchs of the forests; from their feet spring up, as if to enlace them with a magic network, the brilliant passiflora, the vanilla with its intoxicating perfume, the banisteria whose roots seem to have dived into mines of gold and borrowed from thence the color of its petals! Hither the birds of Paradise and Brazilian parrots come to build their nests; here the bluebird and the purple-necked wood-pigeon coo and sing; here, like swarms of bees, thousands of humming-birds of mingled emerald and sapphire, warble and glitter as they suck the nectar from the flowers. This was what you hoped to contemplate, poor Selkirk! and this joy, like many others, is henceforth forbidden.

In his floating prison, in his submarine cell, his only employment is to listen to the dashing of the waves against the ship, or now and then to catch a glimpse of the blue sky through the hatchways.

What cares he? He does not complain; he has learned to abhor mankind, and he loves to be alone, in company with himself and his own thoughts.

Several days passed in this manner.

One morning he felt the brig slacken its speed; the dashing of the wave against the prow diminished, and the Swordfish, suddenly furling its sails, after having slightly rocked hither and thither, stopped. They had just cast anchor. Where? he knows not.

Soon he hears the rattling of the rope-ladder which serves as a stairway to those above who would communicate with his prison. They come, on the part of the captain, to seek him.

He finds the latter seated on the deck, surrounded by his principalmen.

'Young man,' said Stradling, 'I have been obliged to be severe for the sake of an example; but you have been sufficiently punished by the time you have passed below there,'—and he pointed to the ship's hold. 'Now, your wish shall be granted. You shall be allowed to land.'

And the rare smile which sometimes hovered on his lips, stole over his rigid face.

'So much the better,' replied Selkirk, laconically.

The boat was let down; he entered it, and ten minutes afterwards disembarked on a green shore, where the waves, as they broke upon it, seemed to murmur softly in his ear the word, *liberty*!

The boat immediately rejoined the ship, which set sail, coasted along Chili and Patagonia, and re-entered the Northern Sea by the Straits of Magellan.

CHAPTER IV.

Inspection of the Country.—Marimonda.—A City seen through the Fog. —The Sea every where.—Dialogue with a Toucan.—The first Shot. — Declaration of War.—Vengeance.—A Terrestrial Paradise.

While watching the departure of the Swordfish, Alexander Selkirk felt the same sensation as on that day when he had seen the doors of the college of St. Andrew thrown open for his exit; once more he was his own master. Now, however, it is at some thousands of miles from his country that he must reap the benefits of his independence, and this idea embitters his emotions of joy.

But is he not about to find countrymen at Coquimbo? And if their society should be unpleasing?—if their habits, their mode of life, their persons, should become objects of antipathy to the misanthropic Selkirk, as it is but natural to fear? Well! after all, no engagement binds him to them; he will be always free to enter, in the capacity of a sailor, the first vessel which may leave for Europe.

Determined to act as shall seem good to him,—to make some excursions into the interior of the continent, if an opportunity presents itself, and he will know how to make one,—he casts a first glance at the land of his adoption.

Before him extends a vast shore, studded with groves of trees, covered with fine turf and little flowers joyfully unfolding their petals to the sun: two streams, having their source at the very base of the opposite hills, after having meandered around this immense lawn, unite almost at his feet.

He bends down to one of these streams, fills the hollow of his hand with water, and tastes it, as a libation, and as a toast to the generous land which has just received him; the water is excellent; he plucks a flower, and continues his inspection.

On his left rise high mountains, terraced and verdant, excepting at their summits, on one of which he perceives a goat, with long horns, stationed there immovable like a sentinel, and whose delicate profile is clearly defined on the azure of the sky. On the side towards the sea, the mountains, bending their gray and naked heads, resemble stone giants, watching the movements of the wave which dashes at their feet.

On his right, where the land declines, he sees little valleys linked together with charming undulations; but on the mountains at his left, in the valleys at his right, among the hills in the distance, his eye vainly seeks the vestige of a human habitation.

He sets out in search of one. The boat from which he landed has deposited on the shore his effects—his arms, his nautical instruments, his charts, a Bible, and provisions of various kinds. Notwithstanding his piratical sentiments, the captain of the Swordfish has not designed to precede exile by confiscation. Selkirk takes his gun, his gourd; but, unable to carry all his riches, he conceals them behind a stony thicket, well defended by the darts of the cactus, and the sword-like leaves of the aloe, not caring to have the first comer seize them as his booty.

As he is occupied with this duty, he feels himself suddenly clasped by two long hairy arms; he turns his head, it is Marimonda, the captain's monkey, a female of the largest species.

How came she there? Selkirk does not know.

Disgusted with her sea-voyages, with the intelligence natural to her race, Marimonda has undoubtedly profited by the moment of the boat's leaving the ship to conceal herself in it and gain the shore along with the prisoner, which she might easily have done, unseen by all, during the transporting of the effects and provisions.

However this may be, Selkirk begins by freeing himself from her grasp, repulses the monkey and sets out: but the latter perseveres in following, and after having, by her most graceful grimaces, sought to conciliate him, marches beside him. Not caring to arrive at Coquimbo escorted by such a companion, which would give him in a city the appearance of a mountebank and showman of monkeys, Selkirk, this time, repulses her rudely, not with his hand, but with the butt of his gun.

Struck in the breast by this home thrust, the poor monkey stops, rolls up her eyes, moves her lips, and growling confusedly her complaints and reproaches, crouches beneath a tuft of the sapota, leaving the man to pursue his way alone.

Selkirk has at first directed his steps toward the valleys; after having traversed these, he arrives at the margin of a sandy plain, and as far as the eye can reach, perceives neither city, village, house, tent nor hut, nothing which can indicate the presence of inhabitants.

Nevertheless, a little grove which he has just traversed, seems to have recently, in its principal path, passed under the shears of a gardener; the foliage presents a certain symmetry; fragments of branches are strewed, on the ground, which seem to have been freshly cut; he even thinks he sees vestiges of the passage of a flock. On the lawn of the shore, he has seen, and still sees around him, trees with tufted heads, which must owe this form to art. He continues his researches.

At last, in the distance, beneath a fog which is just beginning to dissolve, he perceives a vast mass of white and red houses, some with terraced roofs, others covered with thatch; through the humid veil which envelopes them, he sees the glistening of the glass in the windows; already he hears at his feet the confused noise of cities; murmuring voices reply; the measured sound of hammers and of mills even reaches his ear.

It is Coquimbo! he cannot doubt it, and shortening his route by a path across the hill, he quickens his pace.

Meanwhile an east wind arises, the fog disappears; when he thinks he has reached the suburbs of the city, Selkirk sees before him only an irregular assemblage of calcareous stones, crowned with dry herbs, or reddish, arid, angular rocks, flattened at their summits, tessellated with fragments of silex and mica, on which the sun is just pouring his rays; a company of goats, which the mist had condemned to a momentary repose, are bounding here and there, startling flocks of clamorous black-birds and plaintive sea-gulls; the fearless and yellow-crested woodpeckers alone do not stir, but continue to hammer with their sharp beaks at some old stunted trees.

The disenchantment is painful for our sailor; the fog has deceived him with the semblance of a city, as it has more than once deluded us in the midst of plains and woods, by the appearance of an ocean with its white waves, its great capes, its bold shores, and its vessels at anchor.

Perhaps Coquimbo is still beyond. Fearing to lose himself if he ventures farther in an unknown land, he resolves to explore it first by a look. Returning to the shore upon which he had landed, he scales the mountains on the north, reaches the first platform, and from thence seeks to discover some indications of a city. Nothing! he still ascends, the circle enlarges around him, but with no better result. Summoning all his courage, through a thousand difficulties, climbing, drawing himself up by the arid and abrupt rocks, piled one upon another, he at last attains a culminating point of the mountain. He can now embrace with his eye an immense horizon, but this immense horizon is the sea! On his right, on his left, before him, behind him, every where the sea!

He is not on the continent, but on an island.

This evening, exhausted with fatigue, he lies down in a grotto at the foot of the mountain, where he passes a night full of agitation and anxiety.

Rising with the sun, his first care, the next morning, is to examine his riches and his provisions. He returns to the thicket of cactus and aloes.

Besides two guns, two hatchets, a knife, an iron pot, a Bible and nautical instruments, all articles belonging to him, he finds there a quantity of nails, a large fragment of a sail, several horns of powder and shot; a bag of ship biscuit, a salted quarter of pork, a little cask of pickled fish, and a dozen cocoa-nuts.

The night before, at sight of these articles, he had supposed a sentiment of justice and humanity to exist in the soul of the corsair. Just now, he had said to himself that Stradling, deceived by a false reckoning of latitude, had landed him on an island, perhaps believing it to be a projecting shore of the continent. Now, the abundance of his supplies, this biscuit, these salt provisions, these fruits of the cocoa, all valueless if he had really landed at Coquimbo, lead him to suspect that the vindictive Englishman has designedly chosen the place of his exile.

But this exile, is it complete isolation? Is the island inhabited or deserted? If it is inhabited, as he still believes he has reason to suppose, by whom is it so?

That he may obtain a reply to this double question, he resolves to traverse the country in its whole extent. At the very commencement of his journey, the immobility of a bird suffices to give to the doubt, on which his thoughts vacillate, the appearance almost of a certainty.

This bird is a toucan, of brilliant plumage and monstrous beak. Selkirk passes near it, with his eyes fixed on the branch which serves as a perch, and the toucan, without stirring, looks at him with a species of calm and placid astonishment.

Selkirk stops; he comprehends the mute language of the bird.

'You do not know then what a man is! He is the enemy of every creature to whom God has given life, the enemy even of his kind! You have then never been threatened by the arms that I bear!'

And with the palm of his hand, striking the butt of his gun, he made the hammer click.

At the sound of his voice, as at the noise of the hammer, the bird raised its head, manifesting new and redoubled surprise, but without any other movement. It seemed to think that the man and the gun were one, and that its strange interlocutor possessed two different voices.

At last, by way of reply, it uttered a few shrill and prolonged cries, accompanied by the rattling of its two horny mandibles. After which, acting the great nobleman, cutting short the audience he has deigned to grant, the toucan is silent, turns its head, proudly raises one of its wings and busies itself in smoothing, with the point of its large beak, its beautiful greenish feathers, variegated with purple.

At some distance from this spot, still following the margin of a wooded hill, Selkirk sees other birds, some in their nests, others warbling in the shade; all manifesting no more alarm at his presence than did the toucan. Crested orioles, hooded bullfinches, alight to pick up little grains or insects almost at his feet; humming-birds, variegated cotingas, red manaquins flutter before him in the sunbeams, pursuing invisible flies; little wood-peckers, black or green, hop around the trunks of the trees, stopping a moment to see him pass and then resuming their spiral ascent.

The confidence which he inspires is not confined to these winged people. Upon a hillock of turf he perceives an animal, with pointed nose, brown fur enamelled with red spots, and of the size of a hare; seated on its hind paws, longer than those in front, it uses these, after the manner of squirrels, to carry to its mouth some nuts of the maripa, which constitute its breakfast. It is an agouti,[1] a mother, her little ones are near. At sight of the stranger they run to her, but quickly re-assured, quietly finish their morning repast.

Farther on, coatis,[2] with short ears, and long tails; companies of little Guinea pigs; armadillos, a species of hedge-hog without the quills, but covered with an armor of scales, more compact and impervious than that of the ancient knights of the Middle Ages, arrange themselves along the line of his route, as if to pass him in review.

[1]

Agouti. An animal of the bigness of a rabbit, with bright red hair, and a little tail without hair. He has but two teeth in each jaw; holds his meat in his forepaws like a squirrel, and has a very remarkable cry: when he is angry, his hair stands on end, and he strikes the earth with his hind feet; and when chased, he flies to a hollow tree, whence he is expelled by smoke.—*Trevoux*.

[2]

The *coati* is a native of Brazil, not unlike the racoon in the general form of the body, and, like that animal, it frequently sits up on the hinder legs, and in this position carries its food to its mouth. If left at liberty in a state of tameness, it will pursue poultry, and destroy every living thing that it has strength to conquer. When it sleeps it rolls itself into a lump, and remains immovable for fifteen hours together. His eyes are small, but full of life; and when domesticated, this creature is very playful and amusing. A great peculiarity belonging to this animal is the length of his snout, which resembles in some particulars the trunk of the elephant, as it is movable in every direction. The ears are round, and like those of a rat; the forefeet have five toes each. The hair is short and rough on the back, and of a blackish color; the tail is marked with rings of black, like the wild cat; the rest of the animal is a mixture of black and red.

Alas! this general quiet does but deepen in the heart of Selkirk the certainty of his isolation.

Nevertheless, yesterday, said he to himself, in this thick wood, did I not see alleys trimmed with the shears, trees shaped by the pruning-knife?

And the little grove which he visited the evening previous, at that instant presents itself before him. He examines the trees; they are myrtles of various heights; but among their glossy branches, he in vain seeks traces of the pruning-knife or shears; nature alone has thus disposed in spheroids or umbels the extremities of this rich vegetation.

The same disappointment awaits him in the underwood. The only pruners have been goats, or other animals, daintily cropping the green shoots.

Then only does the complete and terrible certainty of his disaster fall on him and crush him. Behold him blotted from the number of men, perhaps condemned to die of misery and of hunger! more securely imprisoned, more entirely forgotten by the world than the most hardened criminal plunged in the lowest depths of the Bastile! He at least, has a jailor! Miserable Stradling!

At this moment he hears a noise above his head: it is the monkey.

Marimonda, on her side, has also inspected the island; she has already tasted its productions. Whether she is satisfied with her discoveries, or whether forgiveness and forgetfulness of injuries are natural to her, on perceiving her old companion, wagging her head in token of good-will, she descends towards him from the tree on which she is perched.

But Marimonda is the captain's monkey; she has been his property, his favorite, his flatterer! In the disposition of mind in which Selkirk finds himself, he does not need these thoughts to make him pitiless. Marimonda reminds him of Stradling; the monkey shall pay for the man!

He lowers his gun, and fires. The monkey has seen the movement and divined his intentions; she has only time to retreat behind her tree, which does not prevent her receiving in her side a part of the charge.

This detonation of fire-arms, the first perhaps which has resounded in this corner of the earth since the creation of the world, as it is prolonged from echo to echo, even to the highest mountains, awakens in every part of the island as it were a groan of distress. Instinct, that sublime prescience, has revealed to all that a great peril has just been born.

To the cries of affright from birds of every species, to the uneasy and distant bleating of the goats, succeeds a plaintive moaning, like the voice of a wailing infant.

It is Marimonda lamenting over her wound.

At nightfall, after an entire day of walks and explorations, Selkirk is returning to his grotto on the shore, when he sees a stone fall at his feet, then another.

While he, astonished, is seeking to divine the direction from which this invisible battery plays, a little date-stone hits him on the cheek. He immediately hears as it were a joyous whistling in the foliage, which is agitated at his right, and sees Marimonda leaping from tree to tree, using for this movement her feet, her tail, and one hand; for she holds the other to her side. It is a compress on her wound.

War is already in the island! Selkirk has a declared enemy here! And this island, is it deserted? He has just traversed it in every direction without seeing any thing which betokens the existence of a human being.

His disaster is then complete; henceforth not a doubt of it can exist. And yet his forehead wears rather the character of hope and fortitude than of discouragement; it is more than resignation, it is pride.

He has just visited his empire. The island, irregular in form, is from four to five leagues in length; in breadth it is from one and a half to two leagues. This abode to which he is condemned, is the most enchanting retreat he could have chosen; a luxuriant park cradled upon the waves.

If sometimes, in the mountainous parts, he has encountered sterile and rugged rocks, even abysses and precipices, they seem to be placed there only as a contrast to the fresh and green valleys which encircle them. If he has seen some dark, dense, inaccessible forests, entangled in the thousand arms of interwoven vines, he has not discovered a single reptile.

Every where, springs of living water, little streams which are lost under a thick verdure, or fall in cascades from the summits of the hills; every where a luxuriant vegetation; esculent and refreshing plants, celery, cresses, sorrel, spring in profusion beneath his feet; over his head, and almost within reach of his hand, palm-cabbages, and unknown fruits of succulent appearance: on the margin of the shores, muscles, periwinkles, shell-fish of every species, crabs crawling in the moist sand; beneath the transparent waters, innumerable shoals of fishes of all colors, all forms. Will game be wanting here? After what he has seen this morning, he will not even need his gun to obtain it. Oh! his provision of powder will last him a long time.

What has he to desire more in this terrestrial Paradise? The society of men? Why? That he may find a master, a chief, under whose will he must bend? Men! but he despises, detests them! Is he not then sufficient for himself? Yes! this shall be his glory, his happiness! To live in entire liberty, to depend only upon himself, will not this impart to his soul true dignity? Besides, this island cannot be so far from the coast, but, from time to time, ships, or at least boats must come in sight. This is then for him but a transient seclusion; but were he even condemned to eternal isolation, this isolation has ceased to terrify him, he accepts it! Has he not almost always lived alone, in spirit at least? When he was in the depths of the hold, was he not better satisfied with his fate than when surrounded by those coarse sailors who composed the worthy crew of the Swordfish?

To-day he is no longer the prisoner of Stradling, he is the prisoner of God! and this thought reassures him.

A sailor, he has never loved but the sea; well! the sea surrounds him, guards him! He has then only thanks to render to God.

Arrived at his grotto, he takes his Bible, opens it; but the sun, suddenly sinking below the horizon, permits him to read only this passage on which his finger is placed: 'Thou shalt perish in thy pride!'

CHAPTER V.

Labors of the Colonist.—His Study.—Fishing.—Administration. —Selkirk Island.—The New Prometheus.—What is wanting to Happiness.—Encounter with Marimonda.—Monologue.

Three months have passed away.

Thanks to Selkirk, the shore which received him at his disembarkation, presents to-day an aspect not only picturesque, but animated. The hand of man has made itself felt there.

The bushes and tufts of trees which hid the view of the hills in the distance, have been uprooted and cut down; pretty paths, covered with gravel, wind over the vast lawn; one in the direction of the valleys at the right, another towards the mountains at the left; a third leads to a tall mimosa, whose topmost boughs and dense foliage spread out like a parasol. A wooden bench, composed of some round sticks, driven into the earth, with branches interwoven and covered with bark, surrounds it; a rustic table, constructed in the same manner, stands at the foot of the tree. This is the study and place of meditation of the exile; here also he comes to take his meals, in sight of the sea.

All three paths terminate in the grotto which Selkirk continues to make his residence. This grotto he has enlarged, quarried out with his hatchet, to make room for himself, his furniture, and provisions. He has even attempted to decorate its exterior with a bank of turf, and several species of creeping plants, trained to cover its calcareous nudity. At the entrance of his habitation, rise two young palm-trees, transplanted there by him, to serve as a portico. But nature is not always obedient to man; the vines and palm-trees do not prosper in their new location, and now the long flexible branches of the one, and the broad leaves of the other, droop half withered above the grotto, which they disfigure rather than decorate.

By constant care, and with the aid of his streams, Selkirk hopes to be able to restore them to life and health. He has imposed on his two streams another duty, that of supplying a bed of water-cresses and a fish-pond, both provident establishments, the first of which has succeeded perfectly. As for the second, his most arduous task has been, not to dig the fish-pond, but to people it. For this purpose he has been compelled to become a fisherman, to manufacture a net. He has succeeded, with some threads from his fragment of a sail, the fibres of his cocoa-nuts, and tough reeds, woven in close meshes; unfortunately those fine fishes, breams, eels and angel-fish, which show themselves so readily through the limpid wave, are not as easy to catch as to see. Under the surface, almost at a level with the water, there is a ledge of rocks, upon which the net cannot be managed. After several fruitless attempts, he is obliged to content himself with the insignificant employment of fishing with a line; a nail flattened, sharpened and bent, performs the office of a hook. Success ensues, but only with time and patience; fortunately the sea-crabs allow themselves to be caught with the hand, and the fish-pond does not long remain useless and deserted.

Besides, has not our fortunate Selkirk the resource of hunting? The chase he had commenced generously, like a wise monarch, who wages war only for the general interest. It is true, that as it happens with most wise monarchs, his own private interest is also to be consulted, at least he thinks so.

Wild cats existed in the island, destroying young broods, agoutis, and other small game; he has almost entirely rid it of these pirates, reserving to himself only the right of levying upon his subjects the tribute of blood. He has already signalized his administration by acts of an entirely different nature.

This king without a people, is ignorant in what part of the great ocean, and at what distance from its shores, is situated his nameless kingdom.

Armed with his spy-glass, by the aid of his nautical charts, he attempts to ascertain, by the position of the stars, its longitude and latitude. He at first believes himself to be in one of the islands forming the group of Chiloe; his calculations rectified, he afterwards thinks it the Island of Juan Fernandez, then San Ambrosio, or San Felix. Unable to determine the location exactly, for want of correct instruments, he persuades himself that the country he inhabits has never been surveyed, that it is really a land without a name, and he gives it his own; he calls it Selkirk Island.

Ambitious youth, thou hast thus realized one of thy brightest dreams! Dost thou remember the day when, on the way from Largo to St. Andrew, to join William Dampier, thou didst already see thyself the chief of a new country, discovered and baptized by thee?

Well! has he not more than discovered this country? He inhabits it, he governs it, he reigns in it! Not satisfied with giving his name to the island, he soon creates a special nomenclature for its various localities. To the shore upon which he landed, he gives the name of *Swordfish Beach*; the pile of white and red rocks, which he saw through the fog, is the *False Coquimbo*; he calls *Toucan Forest*, the wood where he saw that bird for the first time; the *Defile of Attack*, is that where Marimonda assaulted him with stones; upon these arid rocks, furrowed by deep ravines and abounding in precipices, he has imposed the odious name of *Stradling*! In his mountains he has the *Oasis*; it is a little shady valley, enlivened by the murmur of a streamlet, and with one extremity opening to the sea. There he often goes to watch the game and the goats, which come to drink at the brook. Above it rises the table-land, with difficulty scaled by him on the day of his arrival, and from whence he became convinced that he had landed on an island. This table-land, he has named *The Discovery*.

The two streams which meander over his lawn, and before his grotto, have also received names. This, commissioned to feed the fish-pond, and which gently warbles through the grass, he calls *The Linnet*; the other, interrupted by little cascades, and whose course is more rapid and impetuous, he calls *The Stammerer*.

He has now destroyed the noxious animals, administered government, opened ways of communication, given a name to every part of his island. How many great rulers have done no more!

But his labors have not been confined to his fish-pond, his bed of water-cresses, his hunting, fishing, building, felling of trees; it has become necessary to procure that essential element of civilization, of comfort, fire.

What could the opulent proprietor of this enchanting abode do without fire? Is it not necessary, if he would open a passage through the dense woods? Is it not indispensable to his kitchen? Some of his trees, it is true, afford fruits in abundance; but most of these fruits are of a dry and woody nature; besides, young and vigorous, easily acquiring an appetite by labor and exercise, can he content himself with a dinner which is only a dessert? Surrounded with fishes of all colors, with feathered and other game, must he then be reduced to dispute with the agoutis, their maripa-nuts?

He reflects; armed with a bit of iron, he strikes the flinty rocks of the mountains, to elicit from them useless sparks. He then remembers that savages obtain fire without flint and matches, by the friction of two pieces of dry wood; he tries, but in vain; he exhausts the strength of his arms, without being discouraged; he tries each tree, wishing even that a thunderbolt might strike the island, if it would leave there a trace of burning. At last, almost discouraged, he attacks the pimento-myrtle; [1] he recommences his customary efforts of rubbing. The twigs grow warm with the friction; a little white smoke appears, fluttering to and fro between his hands, rapid and trembling with emotion. The flame bursts forth! He utters a cry of triumph, and, hastily collecting other twigs and dry reeds, he leaps for joy around his fire, which, like another Prometheus, he has just stolen, not from heaven, but from earth!

[1]

Myrtus aromatica; its berries are known under the name of Jamaica pepper.

Afterwards, in his gratitude, he runs to the myrtle, embraces it, kisses it. An act of folly, perhaps; perhaps an act of gratitude, which ascended higher than the topmost branches of the trees, higher than the culminating summits of the mountains of the island.

But this fire, must he, each time he may need it, go through the same tedious process? Not far from his grotto, in a cavity which a projecting rock protects from the sea breeze, he piles up wood and brush, sets fire to it, keeps it alive from time to time, by the addition of combustibles, and comprehends why, among primitive nations, the earliest worship should have been that of fire; why, from Zoroaster to the Vestals, the care of preserving it should have been held sacred.

At a later period, in the ordinary course of things, he simplified his means of preservation. With some threads and the fat of his game, he contrived a lamp; still later, he had oil, and reeds served him for wicks.

Dating from this moment, the entire island paid tribute to him; the crabs, the eels, the flesh of the agouti, savory like that of the rabbit, by turns figured on his table. When he seasoned them with some morsels of pork, substituting ship biscuit for bread, his repasts were fit for an admiral.

Although the goats had become wild, like the other inhabitants of the island, since all had learned the nature of man, and of the thunder, which he directed at his will, Selkirk still surprised them within gun-shot. Not only was their flesh profitable for food; their horns, long and hollow, served to contain powder and other small articles necessary to his house-keeping; of their skins he made carpets, coverings, and bags to protect his provisions from dampness. He even manufactured a game-pouch, which he constantly carried when hunting.

His salt fish, his biscuit, some well smoked quarters of goat's flesh, and the productions of his fish-pond, at present constitute a store on which he can live for a long time, without any care, but to ameliorate his condition.

He is now in possession of all the enjoyments he has coveted, abundance, leisure, absolute freedom.

And yet, his brow is sometimes clouded, and an unaccountable uneasiness torments him; something seems wanting; his appetite fails, his courage grows feeble, his reveries are painfully prolonged. But, by mature reflection, he has discovered the cause of the evil.

What is it that is so essential to his happiness? Tobacco.

Our factitious wants often exercise over us a more tyrannical empire, than our real ones; it seems as if we clung with more force and tenacity to this second nature, because we have ourselves created it; it originates in us; the other originates with God, and is common to all!

Selkirk now persuades himself that tobacco alone is wanting to his comfort; it is this privation which throws him into these sorrowful fits of languor. If Stradling had only given him a good stock of tobacco, he would have pardoned all; he no longer feels courage to hate him. What to him imports the plenty which surrounds him, if he has no tobacco? of what use is his leisure, if he cannot spend it in smoking? what avails even this fire, which he has just conquered, if he is prevented from lighting his pipe at it?

Careworn and dissatisfied, he was wandering one morning through his domains, with his gun on his shoulder, his hatchet at his belt, when he perceived something dancing on a point of land, shadowed by tall canes.

It was Marimonda.

At sight of her enemy, she darted lightly and rapidly behind a woody hillock. An instant afterwards, he saw her tranquilly seated on the topmost branch of a tree, holding in each of her hands fruits which she was alternately striking against the branch, and against each other, to break their tough envelope.

The sight of Marimonda has always awakened in Selkirk a sentiment of repulsion; she not only reminds him of Stradling, but with her withered cheeks, projecting jaw, and especially her dancing motion, he now imagines that she resembles him; and yet, pausing before her, he contemplates her not without a lively emotion of surprise and interest.

He had already encountered her within gun-shot, when engaged in the destruction of the wild cats, and had asked himself whether he should not reckon her among noxious animals. But then Marimonda, with her hand constantly pressed against her side, was with the other seizing various herbs, which she tasted, bruised between her teeth, and applied to her wound; useless remedies, doubtless, for, grown meagre, her hair dull and bristling, she seemed to have but a few days to live, and Selkirk thought her not worth a charge of powder and shot.

And here he finds her alert and healthy, holding in the same hand which had served as a compress, no longer the plant necessary for her cure, but the fruit desirable for her sustenance.

'What,' said Selkirk to himself, 'in an island where this frightful monkey has never before been, she has succeeded in finding without difficulty the *herba sacra*, that which has restored her to health and strength! and I, Selkirk, who have studied at one of the principal universities of Scotland, I am vainly sighing for the plant which would suffice to render me completely happy! Is instinct then superior to reason? To believe this, would be ingratitude to Providence. Instinct is necessary, indispensable to animals, because they cannot benefit by the traditions of their ancestors. The monkey has consulted her instinct, and it has inspired her; if I consult reason, what will be her counsel? She will advise me to do like the monkey; to seek the herb of which I feel so great a want, or at least to endeavor to substitute for it something analogous; to choose, try, and taste, in short, to follow the example of Marimonda! I will not fail to do so; but it is nature reversed, and, for a man, it is too humiliating to see himself reduced to imitate a monkey!'

CHAPTER VI.

The Hammock.—Poison.—Success.—A Calm under the Tropics.—Invasion of the Island.—War and Plunder.—The Oasis.—The Spy-Glass.—Reconciliation.

Do you see, upon a carpet of fresh verdure, the sandy margin of which is bathed by a caressing wave, that hammock suspended to the branches of those fine trees? What happy mortal, during the heat of the day, is there gently rocked, gently refreshed, by a light sea breeze? It is Selkirk; and this hammock is his sail, attached to his tall myrtles by strips of goat-skin. Perhaps he is resting after the fatigues of the day? No, it is the day of the Lord, and Selkirk now can consecrate the Sabbath to repose. With his eyes half closed, he is inhaling, undoubtedly, the perfume of his myrtles, the soft fragrance of his heliotropes? No, something sweeter still pre-occupies him. Is he dreaming of his friends in Scotland, of his first love? He has never known friendship, and the beautiful Catherine is far from his memory. What is he then doing in his hammock? He is smoking his pipe.

His pipe! Has he a pipe? He has them of all forms, all sizes—made of spiral shells of various kinds, of maripa-nuts, of large reeds; all set in handles of myrtle, stalks of coarse grain, or the hollow bones of birds. In these he is luxurious; he has become a connoisseur; but this has not been the difficulty. Before every thing else, tobacco was wanting.

In consequence of his encounter with Marimonda, he ransacked the woods and meadows, seeking among all plants those which approximated nearest to the nature of the nicotiana. As it was necessary to judge by their taste, he bit their leaves—chewed them, still in imitation of the monkey: but, to his new and profound humiliation, less skilful or less fortunate than the latter, he obtained at first no other result than a sort of poisoning: one of these plants being poisonous.

For several days he saw himself condemned to absolute repose and a spare diet. His mouth, swollen, excoriated, refused all nourishment; his throat was burning; his body was covered with an eruption, and his languid and trembling limbs scarcely permitted him to drag himself to the stream to quench there the thirst by which he was devoured.

He believed himself about to die; and grief then imposing silence on pride, with his eyes turned towards the sea, he allowed a long-repressed sigh to escape his heart. It was a regret for his absent country.

Very soon these alarming symptoms disappeared; his strength returned; his water-cresses and wild sorrel completed the cure. Would he have dared to ask it of the other productions of his island? He had become suspicious of nature; these, at least, he had long known.

Scarcely had he recovered, when the want of tobacco made itself felt anew with more force than ever. What to him imports experiment, what imports danger? Is it not to procure this precious, indispensable herb,—which the world had easily done without for thousands of years?

This time, nevertheless, become more prudent, he no longer addresses himself to the sense of taste; but to odor, to that of smell. He has resolved to dry the different plants which appear to him most proper for the use to which he destines them, and to submit them afterwards to a trial by fire. Will not the smoke which escapes from them easily enable him to discover the qualities which he requires, since it is in smoke that they are to evaporate, if he succeeds in his researches?

Of this grand collection of aromatics, two plants, at last, come off victorious. One is the petunia, that charming flower which at present decorates all our gardens, whence the enemies of tobacco may one day banish it; so it is only with trembling that I here announce its relationship to the nicotiana; the other, which, like the petunia, grows in profusion in the islands as well as on the continent of Southern America, is the herb *coca*, improperly so called, for its precious leaves, which are to the natives of Peru and Chili, what the *betel* is for the Indians of Malabar, grow on an elegant shrub. [1]

[1]

The *erythroxylum coca.*

These two plants, separately or together, composed, thanks to a slight amalgam of chalk, sea-water, and bruised pepper-corns, the most delicious tobacco.

Now, half awake, Selkirk smokes, as he busies himself with constructing some necessary article, such as a ladder, a stool, a basket of rushes, with which he is completing the furniture of his house; he smokes while fishing, and while hunting; on his return to his dwelling, he lies down at the entrance of his grotto, on his bank of turf, re-lights his pipe at his fire, and smokes; at the hour of breakfast or of dinner, seated beneath the shade of his mimosa, his elbow on the table, his Bible open before him, he smokes still.

Well! notwithstanding these pleasures so long desired, notwithstanding this addition to his comfort, notwithstanding his pipe, this vague uneasiness sometimes assails him anew.

He ascribes it to enfeebled health; and yet he remains active and vigorous; he ascribes it to the powerful odors of certain trees which affect his brain. These trees he destroys around him, but his uneasiness continues; he ascribes it to his food, the insipidity of the fish which he has eaten without salt, since his quarter of pork is consumed, and his stores of pickled fish exhausted. In fact, the flesh of fish has for some time given him a nausea, occasioned frequent indigestions; he renounces it; his stomach recovers its tone; but his fits of torpor and melancholy continue.

This state of suffering is most painful at those moments of profound calm, common between the tropics, when the birds are silent, when from the thickets and burrows issue no murmurs, when the insect seems to sleep within the closed corollas of the flowers; when the leaves of the mimosa fold themselves; when the tree-tops are not swayed by the slightest breath of air, and the sea, motionless, ceases to dash against the shore. What an inexpressible weight such a silence adds to isolation! And yet it is not an unbroken silence, for then a shrill and harsh sound seems to grate upon the ear. It is as if in this muteness of nature, one could hear the motion of the earth on its axis; then, above his head, in the depths of immensity, the whirling of the celestial spheres and myriads of worlds which gravitate in space. Thought becomes troubled and exhausted before this overwhelming and terrible immobility, and the man who, at such a moment, cannot have recourse to his kind, to distract or re-assure him, is overpowered with his own insignificance.

Sometimes the solitary calls on himself to break this oppressive and painful silence; he articulates a few words aloud, and his voice inspires him with fear;

it seems formidable and unnatural.

During one of these sinister calms, in which every thing in creation seemed to pause, even the heart of man, seated on the shore, not having even strength to smoke, Selkirk was vainly awaiting the evening breeze; nothing came, but the obscurity of night. The moon, delaying her appearance, submitting in her turn to the sluggishness of all things, seemed detained below the circle of the horizon by some fatal power; the sea was dull, gloomy, and as it were congealed.

Suddenly, though there was not a breath of air, Selkirk saw at his right, on a vast but limited tract of ocean, the waves violently agitated and foaming. He thought he distinguished a multitude of barques and canoes furrowing the surface of the waters; not far from Swordfish Beach, the flotilla enters a little cove running up into the mountains.

He no longer sees any thing; but he hears a frightful tumult of discordant cries.

There is no room for doubt! some Indian tribes, pursued perhaps by new conquerors from Europe, have just disembarked on the shore. Wo to him! he can hope from them neither pity nor mercy. A cold sweat bathes his forehead; he runs to his grotto, takes his gun, puts in his goatskin pouch some horns of powder and shot, a piece of smoked meat, not forgetting his Bible! and passes the night wandering in the woods, in the mountains, a prey to a thousand terrors; hearing without cessation the steps of pursuers behind him, and seeing fiery eyes glaring at him through the thickets.

At day-break, with a thousand precautions, he returns to his grotto. He finds the beach covered with seals.

These were the enemies whose invasion had so alarmed him.

It is now the middle of the month of February, the period of the greatest tropical heats, and these amphibia, having left the shores of Chili or Peru, are accomplishing one of their periodical migrations. They have just taken possession of the island, one of their accustomed stations. But the island has now a master.

Where he expected to encounter a peril, Selkirk finds amusement, a subject of study, perhaps a resource.

A long time ago he has read, in the narratives of voyagers, singular stories concerning these marine animals, these *lions*, these *sea-elephants*, flocks of old Neptune, who have their chiefs, their pacha; who are acquainted with and practise the discipline of war; stationing vigilant sentinels in the spots they occupy, communicating to each other a pass-word, and attentive to the *Qui vive*?

He spies them, he watches them, he takes pleasure in examining their grotesque forms,—half quadruped, half fish; their feet encased in a sort of web, and terminated by crooked claws, with which they creep on the earth; their skins, covered with short and glossy hair; their round heads and eyes.

He is a witness of their sports, their combats; but very soon their frightful roaring and bellowing annoys him, and makes him regret the silence of his solitude. Another cause of complaint against them soon arises.

One morning, Selkirk finds his fish-pond and bed of water-cresses devastated.

Exasperated, he declares war against the invaders: during three days he tracks them, pursues them; ten of them fall beneath his balls, leaving the shore bathed in their blood. The rest at last take flight, and the army of seals, regaining the sea with despairing cries, goes to establish itself at the other extremity of the island.

This war has been profitable to the conqueror. With the skin of the vanquished he makes himself a new hammock, which permits him to employ his sail for other uses; he also makes leather bottles, in which he preserves the oil which he extracts in abundance from their fat. Now he can have a lamp constantly burning, even by night. He has all the comforts of life. Of the hairy skin of the seals, he manufactures a broad-brimmed hat, which shields him from the burning rays of the sun. He tastes their flesh; it appears to him insipid and nauseous, like that of the fish; but the tongue, the heart, seasoned with pepper, are for him quite a luxury.

Days, weeks, months roll away in the same toils, the same recreations. Whatever he may do to drive it away, this apathetic sadness, this sinking of soul, which has already tormented him at different periods, becomes with Selkirk more and more frequent; he cannot conquer it as he did the seals. His seals, he now regrets. When they were encamped on the shore, they at least gave him something to look at, an amusement; something lived, moved, near him.

When he finds himself a prey to these fits, which, in his pride, he persists in attributing to transient indisposition, he goes to walk in the mountains, taking with him only his pipe, his Bible, and his spy-glass.

He often pursues his journey as far as the oasis; there, he seats himself at the extremity of the little valley, opposite the sea, from which his eye can traverse its immense extent. He opens the holy book, and closes it immediately; then, his brow reddening, he seizes his spy-glass, levels it, and remains entire hours measuring the ocean, wave by wave.

What is he looking for there? He seeks a sail, a sail which shall come to his island and bear him from his desert, from his *ennui*. His *ennui* he can no longer dissimulate; this is the evil of his solitude.

One day, while he was at this spot, the setting sun suddenly illuminated a black point, against which the waves seemed to break in foam, as against the prow of a ship; his eyes become dim, a tremor seizes him. He looks again—keeps his glass for a long time fixed on the same object, but the black point does not stir.

'Another illusion!' said he to himself; 'it is a reef, a rock which the tide has left bare.'

He wipes the glasses of his spy-glass, he examines again; he seems to see the waves whiten and whirl for a large space around this rock.

'Can it be an island? If an island, is it inhabited? I will construct a barque, and if God has pity on me I will reach it.'

At this moment he hears footsteps resound on the dry leaves which the wind has swept into the little valley. He turns hastily.

It is Marimonda.

Marimonda has no longer her lively and dancing motions; she also seems languid, sad. At sight of Selkirk, she makes a movement as if to flee; but almost immediately advances a little, and, sorrowful, with bent brow, sits down on a bank not far from him.

Has she then remarked that he is without arms?

On his side, Selkirk who had not met her for a long time, seemed to have forgotten his former aversion.

At all events, is she not the most intelligent being chance has placed near him? He remembers that, in the ship, she obeyed the voice, the gesture of the captain, and that her tricks amused the whole crew. This resemblance to the human form, which he at first disliked, now awakens in him ideas of indulgence and peace. He reproaches himself with having treated her so brutally, when the poor animal, who alone had accompanied him into exile, at first accosted him with a caress. And now she returns, laying aside all ill-will, forgetting even the wound which she received from him in an impulse of irritation and hatred, of which she was not the object, for which she ought not to be responsible.

He therefore makes to her a little sign with the head.

Marimonda replies by winks of the eye and motions of the shoulders, which Selkirk thinks not wholly destitute of grace.

He rises and approaches her, saluting her with an amicable gesture.

She awaits him, chattering with her teeth and lips with an expression of joy.

Selkirk gently passes his hand over her forehead and neck, calling her by name; then he starts for his habitation, and Marimonda follows him. The man and the monkey have just been reconciled. Both were tired of their isolation.

CHAPTER VII.

A Tête-a-tête.—The Monkey's Goblet.—The Palace.—A Removal.—Winter under the Tropics—Plans for the Future.—Property.—A burst of Laughter.—Misfortune not far off.

Tranquility of mind has returned to our solitary; now, his reveries are more pleasant and less prolonged; his walks through the woods, his moments of repose during the heat of the day seem more endurable since *something*, besides his shadow, keeps him company; he has resumed his taste for labor since there is *somebody* to look at him; speech has returned to him since *somebody* replies to his voice. This *somebody*, this *something*, is Marimonda.

Marimonda is now the companion of Selkirk, his friend, his slave; she seems to comprehend his slightest gestures and even his *ennui*. To amuse him, she resorts to a thousand expedients, a thousand tricks of the agility peculiar to her race; she goes, she comes, she runs, she leaps, she bounds, she chatters at his side; she tries to people his solitude, to make a rustling around him; she brings him his pipes, rocks him in his hammock, and, for all these cares, all this attention, demands only a caress, which is no longer refused.

She is often a spectator of her master's repasts; sometimes even shares them. This was at first a favor, afterwards a habit, as in the case of honest countrymen, who, secluded from the world, by degrees admit their servants into their intimacy. Selkirk had not to fear the importunate, unexpected visit of a neighbor or a curious stranger.

So it is in the open air, on the latticed table, in the shade of his great mimosa, that these repasts in common take place; the master occupies the bench, the servant humbly seats herself on the stool, ready, at the first signal, to leave her place and assist in serving. Have we not seen in India, ourang-outangs trained to perform the office of domestics? and Marimonda was in nothing inferior in intelligence and activity.

She is now fond of the flesh of the goat, of that of the coatis and agoutis, for monkeys easily become carnivorous; but the table is also sometimes covered with the products of her hunting. If the dessert fails, she hastily interrupts her repast, leaves the master to continue his alone, buries herself in the surrounding woods, reaches in three bounds the tops of the trees, and quickly returns with a supply of fruits which he can fearlessly taste, for she knows them.

Selkirk was one day a witness of the singular facility with which she could supply her wants.

At the morning repast, seeing him use one of his cocoa-nuts which he had fashioned in the form of a cup to drink from; in her instinct of imitation, she had attempted to seize the cup in her turn; a look of reprimand stopped her short in her attempt. Whether she felt a species of humiliation at being forced to quench her thirst in the presence of her master, by going to the banks of the stream and lapping there, like a vulgar animal; or whether the reprimand had painfully affected her, she abstained from drinking and remained for some time quiet and dreamy; but at the following repast, with lifted head and sparkling eye she resumed her place on the stool, provided with a goblet, a goblet belonging to her, lawfully obtained by her, and, with an air of triumph presented it to Selkirk, who, wondering, did not hesitate an instant to share with the monkey the water contained in his gourd.

This goblet was the ligneous and impermeable capsule, the fruit, naturally and deeply hollowed out, of a tree called *quatela*. [1] It was thus that the intelligent Marimonda, after having borrowed from the numerous vegetables of the island their leaves, to ameliorate her sufferings, to heal her wounds; their fruits for her nourishment and even for her sports, also found means to obtain the divers utensils for house-keeping of which she stood in need.

[1]

> The *lecythis quatela*, of the family of the *lecythidées*, created by Professor Richard, and whose singular fruits bear, in Peru as well as in Chili, the denomination of *monkey's goblets*.

Charmed with her gentleness, her docility, the affection she seemed to bear him, Selkirk grew more and more attached to her. Winter, that is, the rainy season which usually lasts in these regions during the months of June and July, was approaching; he suffered in anticipation, from the idea that during this time his gentle companion would not be able to retain her habitual shelter, beneath the foliage of the trees; he conceived the project of giving up to her his grotto, and constructing for himself a new habitation, spacious and commodious. It is thus that our most generous resolutions, whatever we may design to do, encountering in their way personal interest, often turn to the increase of our own private welfare.

At a little distance from the grotto, but farther inland, on the banks of the stream called the *Linnet*, there was a thicket of verdure shaded by five myrtles of from fifteen to twenty feet in height, and whose stems presented a diameter more than sufficient to insure the solidity of the edifice. Four of these myrtles formed an irregular square; the fifth arose in the midst, or nearly so; but our architect is not very particular. He already sees the principal part of his frame; the myrtles will remain in their places, their roots serving as a foundation. He removes the shrubs, the plants, the brushwood from the thicket, leaving only a heliotrope which, at a later period, may twine around his house and at evening shed its perfumes. He has become reconciled to its fragrance. He trims the trees, cuts off their tops eight feet above the ground, leaving the middle one, which is to sustain the roof, a foot higher; for this roof reeds and palm-leaves furnish all the materials. The walls, made of a solid network of young branches interwoven, and plastered with a mixture of sand, clay, and chopped rushes, he takes care not to build quite to the top, but to leave between them and the roof a little space, where the air can circulate freely through a light trellis formed of branches of the blue willow.

Then, having finished his work in less than a fortnight, he contemplates it and admires it; Marimonda herself seems to share in his admiration, and in her joy climbing up the new building, she begins to leap, to dance on the roof of foliage, which bears her, and thus gives to Selkirk an additional triumph.

He now proceeds to furnish his palace; he transports thither his bed of reeds and his goatskin coverings. How much better will he be sheltered here than under the gloomy vault of his grotto! How has he been able to content himself so long with such an abode, more suitable for a troglodyte or a monkey! He will no longer be obliged to lift up his curtain of vines, and to peep through the fans of his palm-trees, in order to behold the beneficent rays of the new-born day; they will come of themselves to find him and rejoice him at his awakening, as the sea-breezes will at evening breathe on him, to refresh him in his repose.

Already has the interior of his cabin, of his palace, assumed an aspect which charms him; his guns, his hatchets, his spy-glass, his instruments of labor, well polished and shining, suspended in racks, upon wooden pegs, decorate the walls; upon another partition, his assortment of pipes are arranged on a shelf according to their size; on his central pillar, he suspends his game-bag, his gourd, his tobacco-pouch, and various articles of daily use. As for his iron pot, his smoked meat, his stock of skins, and bottles of seal-oil, he leaves them under the guardianship of Marimonda in the grotto which he will now make his store-house, his kitchen: he will not encumber with them his new dwelling.

He now sets himself to prepare new furniture; he will construct a small portable table, two wooden seats, one for himself, the other for Marimonda, when she comes from her grotto to visit his cabin; for he has now a neighborhood. Besides, during the rainy season, they will be forced to dine under cover.

The first rains have commenced, gentle, fertilizing rains, falling at intervals and lovingly drank in by the earth; Selkirk no longer thinks of his table and seats; another project has just taken the place of these, and seems to deserve the precedence.

Marimonda has just returned from a tour in the woods, bringing fruits of all sorts, among them some which Selkirk has never before seen. He tastes them with more care and attention than usual; then, becoming thoughtful, with his chin resting on his hand says to himself: 'Why should I not make these fruits grow at my door, not far from my habitation? Why should I not attempt to improve them by cultivation? This is a very simple and very prudent idea which should have occurred to me long since; but I was alone, absolutely alone; and one loses courage when thinking of self only. A garden, at once an orchard and a vegetable garden, will be at least as useful to me as my fish-pond and bed of water-cresses; I will make one around my cabin; it will set it off and give it a more home-like appearance! Is not the stream placed here expressly to traverse it and water it? Afterwards, if God assist me, I will raise little kids which will become goats and give me milk, butter, cheese! Why have I not thought of this before? It would have been too much to have undertaken at once. I shall then have tame goats; I will also have Guinea-pigs, agoutis, and coatis. My house shall be enlarged, I will have a farm, a dairy! But the time has not yet come; let us first prepare the garden. Why has it not been already prepared? I am impatient to render the earth productive, fruitful by my cares, to walk in the shade of the trees I may plant; it seems to me that I shall be at home there, more than any where else!'

You are right, Selkirk; to possess the entire island, is to possess nothing; it is simply to have permission to hunt, a right of promenade and pasture, which the other inhabitants of the island, quadrupeds or birds, can claim as well as yourself. What is property, without the power of improvement? Can the earth become the domain of a single person, when the true limits of his possessions must always be those of the field which affords him subsistence? Envy not then the happiness of the rich; they are but the transient holders and distributors of the public fortune; we possess, in reality, only that which we can ourselves enjoy; the rest escapes us, and contributes to the well-being of others.

Selkirk comprehends that his streams, his bank of turf, his fish-pond, his bed of water-cresses, his grotto, his cabin, belong to him far otherwise than the twelve or fifteen square leagues of his island; to his private domain he now intends to add a garden, and this garden, this orchard, will be to him an increase of his wealth, since it will aid in the satisfaction of his wants.

The humidity with which the earth begins to be penetrated, facilitates his labors; he sets himself to the work.

Behold him then, now armed with his hatchet, now with a wooden shovel, which he has just manufactured, clearing the ground, digging, transplanting young fruit-trees, or sowing the seeds which he is soon to see spring up and prosper. Every thing grows rapidly in these climates.

When the garden-spot is marked out, dug, sown, planted, not forgetting the kitchen vegetables, and especially the *coca* and *petunia-nicotiana*, Selkirk, with his arms folded on his spade, thanks God with all his heart,—God who has given him strength to finish his work.

He has never felt so happy as when, with his hands behind his back, he walks smoking, among his beds, in which nothing has as yet appeared; but he already sees, in a dream, his trees covered with blossoms; around these blossoms are buzzing numerous swarms of bees; he reflects upon the means of compelling them to yield the honey of which they have just stolen from him the essence. It is a settled thing, on his farm he will have hives! After his bees, still in his dream, come flocks of humming-birds to plunder in their turn. The happy possessor of the garden will exact no tribute from them, but the pleasure of seeing them suspend, by a silken thread, to the leaves of his shrubs, the elegant little boat in which they cradle their fragile brood. Nothing seems to him more beautiful than his embryo garden; here, he is more than the monarch of the island; he is a proprietor!

Thanks to the garden, Selkirk sees with resignation the two long months of the rainy season pass away. When the heavy torrents render the paths impassable, he consoles himself by thinking that they aid in the germination of his seeds, in the rooting of his young plants. Sometimes, between two deluges, he can scarcely find time to procure himself sufficient game; what matters it! he lives on his provisions: he is forcibly detained within; but has he not now good cheer, good company, and occupation, during his leisure hours?

It is now that he completes his furniture. His table and his seats finished, he undertakes to provide for another want, equally indispensable.

Worn out by the weather, and by service, his garments are becoming ragged. He must shield himself from the humidity of the air; where shall he procure materials? Has he not the choice between seal-skins and goat-skins? He gives the preference to the latter, as more pliable, and behold him a tailor, cutting with the point of his knife; as for thread, it is furnished by the fragment of the sail; and two days afterwards, he finds himself flaming in a newsuit.

To describe the delirious stupefaction of Marimonda, when she perceives her master under this strange costume, would be a thing impossible. She finds him almost like herself, clad like her, in a hairy suit. Never tired of looking at him, of examining him curiously, she leaps, she gambols around him, now rolling at his feet, and uttering little cries of joy, now suspended over his head, at the top of the central pillar, and turning her wild and restless eyes. When she has thus inspected him from head to foot, she runs and crouches in a corner, with her face towards the wall, as if to reflect; then, whirling about, returns towards him, picks up on the way the garment he has just laid aside, looking alternately at this and at the other, very anxious to know which of the two really made a part of the person.

After having enjoyed for a few moments the surprise and transports of his companion, Selkirk takes his Bible and his pipe, and, placing the book on the table, bends over it, preparing to read and to meditate. But, whether in consequence of her joyous excitement, or whether she is emboldened by the species of fraternity which costume establishes between them, Marimonda, without hesitation, directs herself to the little shelf, chooses from it a pipe in her turn, places it gravely between her lips, astonished at not seeing the smoke issue from it in a spiral column; and, with an important air, still imitating her master, comes to sit opposite him, with her brow inclined, and her elbow resting on the table.

Willingly humoring her whim, Selkirk takes the pipe from her hands, fills it with his most spicy tobacco, lights it, and restores it to her.

Hardly has Marimonda respired the first breath, when suddenly letting fall the pipe, overturning the table, emitting the smoke through her mouth and nostrils, she disappears, uttering plaintive cries, as if she had just tasted burning lava.

At sight of the poor monkey, thus thrown into confusion, Selkirk, for the first time since his residence in the island, laughs so loudly, that the echo follows the fugitive to the grotto, where she had taken refuge, and is prolonged from the grotto to the *Oasis*, from the Oasis to the summit of the *Discovery*.

The exile has at last laughed, laughed aloud, and, at the same moment, a terrible disaster is taking place without his knowledge; a new war is preparing for him, in which his arms will be useless.

CHAPTER VIII.

A New Invasion.—Selkirk joyfully meets an ancient Enemy.—Combat on a Red Cedar.—A Mother and her Little Ones.—The Flock.—Fête in the Island; Pacific Combats, Diversions and Swings.—A Sail.—The Burning Wood.—Presentiments of Marimonda.

The next morning the sun has scarcely touched the horizon, Selkirk is still asleep, when he is awakened by a sort of tickling at his feet. Thinking it some caress or trick of Marimonda, risen earlier than usual, he half opens his eyes, sees nothing, and places himself again in a posture to continue his nap. The same tickling is renewed, but with more perseverance, and very soon something sharp and keen penetrates to the quick the hard envelope of his heel. The tickling has become a bite.

This time wide awake, he raises his head. His cabin is full of rats!

Near him, a company of them are tranquilly engaged in breakfasting on his coverings and the rushes of his couch; they are on his table, his seats, along his pillow and his walls; they are playing before his door, running hither and thither through the crevices of his roof, multiplying themselves on his rack and shelf; all biting, gnawing, nibbling—some his seal-skin hat, his tobacco-pouch, the bark ornaments of his furniture; others the handles of his tools, his pipes, his Bible, and even his powder-horn.

Selkirk utters a cry, springs from his couch, and immediately crushes two under his heels. The rest take flight.

As he is pursuing these new invaders with the shovel and musket, he perceives at a few paces' distance Marimonda, sorrowful and drooping, perched on the strong branch of a sapota-tree. By her piteous and chilly appearance, her tangled and wet hair, he doubts not but she has passed the whole night exposed to the inclemency of the weather. But he at first attributes this whim only to her ill-humor the evening before.

On perceiving him, Marimonda descends, from her tree, sad, but still gentle and caressing, and with gestures of terror, points to the grotto. He runs thither.

Here another spectacle of disorder and destruction awaits him; the rats are collected in it by thousands; his furs, his provisions of fruit and game, his bottles formerly filled with oil, every thing is sacked, torn in pieces, afloat; for the water has at last made its way through the crevices of the mountain. To put the climax to his misfortune, his reserve of powder, notwithstanding its double envelope of leather and horn, attacked by the voracious teeth of his aggressors, is swimming in the midst of an oily slime.

The solitary now possesses, for the purpose of hunting, for the renewal of these provisions so necessary to his life, only the few charges contained in his portable powder-horn, and in the barrels of his guns. The blow which has just struck him is his ruin! and still the hardest trial appointed for him is yet to come.

In penetrating the ground, the rains of winter have driven the rats from their holes; hence their invasion of the cabin and the grotto.

Against so many enemies, what can Selkirk do, reduced to his single strength?

He succeeds, nevertheless, in killing some; Marimonda herself, armed with the branch of a tree, serves as an ally, and aids him in putting them to flight; but their combined efforts are ineffectual. An hour after, the accursed race are multiplying round him, more numerous and more ravenous than ever.

He comprehends then what an error he has committed in the complete destruction of the wild cats which peopled the island. With the most generous intentions, how often is man mistaken in the object he pursues! We think we are ridding us of an enemy, and we are depriving ourselves of aprotector. God only knows what he does, and he has admitted apparent evil, as a principle, into the admirable composition of his universe; he suffers the wicked to live. Selkirk had been more severe than God, and he repents it. If his poor cats had only been exiled, he would hasten to proclaim a general amnesty. Alas! there is no amnesty with death. But has he indeed destroyed all? Perhaps some still exist in those distant regions which have already served as a refuge for that other banished race, the seals.

The rains have ceased; the storms of winter, always accompanied by overpowering heat and dense fogs, no longer sadden the island by anticipated darkness, or the gloomy mutterings of continual thunder. The sun, though *garué*[1] absorbs the remainder of the inundation. Followed by Marimonda, Selkirk, for the first time, has ventured to the woods and thickets between the hills beyond the shore and the False Coquimbo, when a sound, sweeter to his ear than would have been the songs of a siren, makes him pause suddenly in ecstasy: it is the mewing of a cat.

[1]

In Peru and Chili, they call *garua* that mist which sometimes, and especially after the rainy season, floats around the disk of the sun.

This cat, strongly built, with a spotted and glossy coat, white nose, and brown whiskers, is stationed at a little distance, on a red cedar, where she is undoubtedly watching her prey.

She is an old settler escaped from the general massacre; the last of the vanquished; perhaps!

Without hesitation, Selkirk clasps the trunk of the tree, climbs it, reaches the first branches; Marimonda follows him and quickly goes beyond. At the aspect of these two aggressors, like herself clad in skin, the cat recoils, ascending; the monkey follows, pursues her from branch to branch, quite to the top of the cedar. Struck on the shoulder with a blow of the claw, she also recoils, but descending, and declaring herself vanquished in the first skirmish, immediately gives over the combat, or rather the sport, for she has seen only sport in the affair.

Selkirk is not so easily discouraged; this cat he must have, he must have her alive; he wishes to make her the guardian of his cabin, his protector against the rats. Three times he succeeds in seizing her; three times the furious animal, struggling, tears his arms or face. It is a terrible, bloody conflict, mingled with exclamations, growlings, and frightful mewings. At last Selkirk, forgetting perhaps in the ardor of combat the object of victory, seizes her vigorously by the skin of the neck, at the risk of strangling her; with the other hand he grasps her around the body. The difficulty is now to carry her. Fortunately he has his game-bag. With one hand he holds her pressed against the fork of the tree; with the other arm he reaches his game-bag, opens it; the conquered animal, half dead, has not made, during this manoeuvre, a single movement of resistance. But when the hunter is about to close it, suddenly rousing herself with a leap, distending by a last effort all her muscles at once, she escapes from his grasp, and precipitates herself from the top of the cedar, to the great terror of Marimonda, then peaceably crouched under the tree, whom the cat brushes against in falling, and to the great disappointment of Selkirk, who thinks he has the captive in his pouch.

Sliding along the trunk, Selkirk descends quickly to the ground; but the enemy has already disappeared, and left no trace. In vain his eyes are turned on all sides; he sees nothing, neither his adversary nor Marimonda, who has undoubtedly fled under the impression of this last terror.

As he is in despair, a whistling familiar to his ear is heard, and at two hundred paces distant he perceives, on an eminence of the False Coquimbo, his monkey, bent double, in an attitude of contemplation, appearing very attentive to what is passing beneath her, and changing her posture only to send a repeated summons to her master.

At all hazards he directs himself to this quarter.

What a spectacle awaits him! In a cavity at the foot of the eminence where Marimonda is, he finds, crouching, still out of breath with her struggle and her race, his fugitive. She is a mother! and six kittens, already active, are rolling in the sun around her.

Selkirk, seizing his knife, kills the mother, and carries off the little ones.

A short time after, the rats have deserted the shore. But their departure, though it prevents the evil they might yet have done, does not remedy that already accomplished.

The provisions of the solitary are almost entirely destroyed, and the little powder which remains is scarcely sufficient for a reserve which he no longer knows where to renew.

The moment at last comes when he possesses no other ammunition than the only charge in his gun. This last charge, his last resource, oh! how preciously he preserves it to-day. While it is there, he can still believe himself armed, still powerful; he has not entirely exhausted his resources; it is his last hope. Who knows?—perhaps he may yet need it to protect his life in circumstances which he cannot foresee.

But since his gun must remain suspended, inactive, to the walls of his cabin, it is time to think of supplying the place of the services it has rendered; it is time to realize his dream, and, according to the usual course of civilization, to substitute the life of a farmer and shepherd for that of a hunter.

Already is his colony augmented by six new guests, domesticated in his house; already, on every side, his seeds are peeping out of the ground under the most favorable auspices; his young trees, firmly rooted, are growing rapidly beneath the double influence of heat and moisture; at the axil of some of their leaves, he sees a bud, an earnest of the harvest. He must now occupy himself with the means of surprising, seizing and retaining the ancestors of his future flock.

Here, patience, address or stratagem can alone avail.

Notwithstanding his natural agility, he does not dream of reaching them by pursuit. Since his last hunts, goats and kids keep themselves usually in the steep and mountainous parts of the island. To leap from rock to rock, to attempt to vie with them in celerity and lightness appears to him, with reason, a foolish and impracticable enterprise. Later, perhaps,... Who knows?

He manufactures snares, traps; but suspicion is now the order of the day around him; each holds himself on the *qui vive*. After long waiting without any result, he finds in his snares a coati, some little Guinea pigs; here is one resource, undoubtedly, but he aims at higher game, and the kids will not allow themselves to be taken by his baits.

He remembers then, that in certain parts of America, the hunters, in order to seize their prey living, have recourse to the lasso, a long cord terminated by a slip-noose, which they know how to throw at great distances, and almost always with certainty.

With a thread which he obtains from the fibres of the aloe, with narrow strips of skin, closely woven, he composes a lasso more than fifty feet long; he tries it; he exercises it now against a tuft of leaves detached from a bush, now against some projecting rock; afterwards he tries it upon Marimonda, who often enough, by her agility and swiftness, puts her master at fault.

In the interval of these preparatory exercises, Selkirk occupies himself with the construction of a latticed inclosure, destined to contain the flock which he hopes to possess; he makes it large and spacious, that his young cattle may bound and sport at their ease; high, that they may respect the limits he assigns them. In one corner, supported by solid posts, he builds a shed, simply covered with branches; that his flock may there be sheltered from the heat of the day. The inclosure and the shed, together with his garden, form a new addition to his great settlement.

When, his kids shall have become goats, when the epoch of domesticity shall have arrived for them, when they shall have contracted habits of tameness, when they have learned to recognize his voice, then, and then only, will he permit them to wander and browse on the neighboring hills, under the direction of a vigilant guardian. This guardian, where shall he find? Why may it not be Marimonda? Marimonda, to whose intelligence he knows not where to affix bounds!

Dreams, dreams, perhaps! and yet but for dreams, but for those gentle phantoms which he creates, and by which he surrounds himself, what would sustain the courage of the solitary?

When Selkirk thinks he has acquired skill in the use of the lasso, he buries himself among the high mountains situated towards the central part of his island. Several days pass amid fruitless attempts, and when the delicately-carved foliage of the mimosa announces, by its folding, that night is approaching, he regains his cabin, gloomy, care-worn, and despairing of the future.

Meanwhile, by his very failures, he has acquired experience. One evening, he returns to his dwelling, bringing with him two young kids, with scarcely perceptible horns, and reddish skin, varied with large brownspots. Marimonda welcomes her new guests, and this evening all in the habitation breathes joy and tranquillity.

The week has not rolled away, when the number of Selkirk's goats exceeds that of his cats; and he takes pleasure in seeing them leap and play together in his inclosure; his mind has recovered its serenity.

'Yes,' said he, with pride, 'man can suffice for himself, can depend on himself only for subsistence and welfare! Am I not a striking proof? Did not all seem lost for me, when an unforeseen catastrophe destroyed the remnant of the provision of powder which I owed to the pity of that miserable captain? Ah! undoubtedly according to his hateful calculations, he had limited the term of my life to the last charge which my gun should contain; this last charge is still there! Of what use will it be to me? Why do I need it? Are not my resources for subsistence more certain and numerous to-day than before? What then is wanting? The society of a Stradling and his fellows? God keep me from them! The best member of the crew of the brig Swordfish came away when I did. I have received from Marimonda more proofs of devotion than from all the companions I have had on land and on sea. What have I to regret? I am well off here; may God keep me in repose and health!'

After this sally, he thought of his hives, which were still wanting, and of the methods to be employed to seize a swarm of bees.

A month after, Selkirk, who religiously kept his reckoning on the margin of his Bible, resolved to celebrate the New Year. It was now the first of January, 1706.

On this day he dined, not in his cabin, nor under his tree, but in the middle of the inclosure, surrounded by his family; fruits and good cheer were more abundant than usual; Marimonda, as was her custom, dined at the same table with himself: the cats shared in the feast; the goats roved around, stretching up to gaze with their blue eyes on the baskets of fruits, and returning to browse on the grass beneath the feet of the guests. Selkirk, as the master of the house, and chief of the family, generously distributed the provisions to his young and frolicksome republic, and Marimonda assisted him as well as she could, in doing the honors.

After the repasts, there were races and combats; the remains of the baskets were thrown to the most skilful and the most adroit; then came, diversions and swings.

Lying in his hammock, where he smoked his most excellent tobacco in his best pipe, Selkirk smilingly contemplated the capricious bounds, the riotous sports of his cats and kids, their graceful postures, their fraternal combats, in which sheathed claws and the inoffensive horn were the only weapons used on either side.

To give more variety to the fête, Marimonda developes all the resources of her daring suppleness; she leaps from right to left, clearing large spaces with inconceivable dexterity. Attaining the summit of a tree, she whistles to attract her master's attention, then, with her two fore-paws clasped in her hind ones, she rolls herself up like a ball and drops on the ground; the foliage crackles beneath her fall, which seems as if it must be mortal; for her, this is only sport. Without altering the position of her limbs, she suddenly stops in her rapid descent, by means of her prehensile tail, that fifth hand, so powerful, with which nature has endowed the monkeys of America. Then, suspended by this organ alone, she accelerates her motions to and fro with incredible rapidity, quickly unwinds her tail from the branch by which she is suspended, and with a dart, traversing the air as if winged, alights at a hundred paces distance on a vine, which she instantly uses as a swing.

Selkirk is astonished; he applauds the tricks of Marimonda, the sports and combats of his other subjects. Meanwhile, his eyes having turned towards the sea, his brow is suddenly overclouded. At the expiration of a few moments of an uneasy and agitated observation, he utters an exclamation, springs from his hammock, runs to his cabin, then to the shore, where he prostrates himself with his hands clasped and raised towards heaven.

He has just perceived a sail.

Provided with his glass, he seeks the sail upon the waves, he finds it. 'It is without doubt a barque,' said he to himself; 'a barque from the neighboring island, or some point of the continent!' And looking again through his copper tube, he clearly distinguishes three masts well rigged, decorated with white sails, which are swelling in the east wind, and gilded by the oblique rays of the declining sun.

'It is a brig! The Swordfish, perhaps! Yes, Stradling has prolonged his voyage in these regions. The time which he had fixed for my exile has rolled away! He is coming to seek me. May he be blessed!'

The movement which the brig made to double the island, had increased more and more the hopes of Selkirk, when the Spanish flag, hoisted at the stern, suddenly unfolded itself to his eyes.

'The enemy!' exclaimed he; 'woe is me! If they land on this coast, whither shall I fly, where conceal myself? In the mountains! Yes, I can there succeed in escaping them! But, the wretches! they will destroy my cabin, my inclosure, my garden! the fruit of so much anxiety and labor!'

And, with palpitating heart, he again watches the manoeuvres of the brig. The latter, having tacked several times, as if to get before the wind, hastily changed her course and stood out to sea.

Selkirk remains stupefied, overwhelmed. ‘These are Spaniards,’ murmured he, after a moment’s hesitation; ‘what matters it! Am I now their enemy? I am only a colonist, an exile, a deserter from the English navy. They owe me protection, assistance, as a Christian. If they required it, I would serve on board their vessel! But they have gone; what method shall I employ to recall them, to signalize my presence?’

There was but one; it was to kindle a large fire on the shore or on the hill. He needs hewn wood, and his supplies are exhausted; what is to bedone?

For an instant, in his disturbed mind, the idea arises to tear the lattice-work from his inclosure, the pillars and the roof from his shed, to pile them around his cabin, and set fire to the whole.

This idea he quickly repulses, but it suffices to show what passed in the inner folds of the heart of this man, who had just now forced himself to believe that happiness was yet possible for him.

On farther reflection, he remembers that behind his grotto, on one of the first terraces of the mountain, there is a dense thicket, where the trees, embarrassed with vines and dry briers, closely interwoven, calcined by the burning reflections of the sun on the rock which surrounds them, present a collection of dead branches and mouldy trunks, scarcely masked by the semblance of vegetation.

Thither he transports all the brands preserved under the ashes of his hearth; he makes a pile of them; throws upon it armfuls of chips, bark and leaves. The flame soon runs along the bushes which encircle the thicket; and, when the sun goes down, an immense column of fire illuminates all this part of the island, and throws its light far over the ocean.

Standing on the shore, Selkirk passes the night with his eyes fixed on the sea, his ear listening attentively to catch the distant sound of a vessel; but nothing presents itself to his glance upon the luminous and sparkling waves, and amid their dashing he hears no other sound but that of the trees and vines crackling in the flames.

At morning all has disappeared. The fire has exhausted itself without going beyond its bounds, and the sea, calm and tranquil, shows nothing upon its surface but a few flocks of gulls.

A week passes away, during which Selkirk remains thoughtful and taciturn; he rarely leaves the shore; he still beholds the sports of his cats and his kids, but no longer smiles at them; Marimonda, by way of amusing him, renews in his presence her surprising feats, but the attention of the master is elsewhere.

Nevertheless, he cannot allow himself time to dream long with impunity; his reserve of smoked beef is nearly exhausted; to save it, he has again resorted to the shell-fish, which his stomach loathes; to the sea-crabs, of which he is tired; he needs other nourishment to restore his strength. He shakes off his lethargy, takes his lasso, his game-bag. His plan now is, not to hunt the kids, but the goats themselves.

As he is about to set out, Marimonda approaches, preparing to accompany him. In his present frame of mind, Selkirk wishes to be alone, and makes her comprehend, by signs, that she must remain at home and watch the flock; but this time, contrary to her custom, she does not seem disposed to obey. Notwithstanding his orders, she follows him, stops when he turns, recommences to follow him, and, by her supplicating looks and expressive gestures, seeks to obtain the permission which he persists in refusing. At last Selkirk speaks severely, and she submits, still protesting against it by her air of sadness and depression. Was this, on her part, caprice or foresight? No one has the secret of these inexplicable instincts, which sometimes reveal to animals the presence of an invisible enemy, or the approach of a disaster.

At evening, Selkirk had not returned! Marimonda passed the night in awaiting him, uttering plaintive cries.

On the morrow the morning rolled away, then the day, then the night, and the cabin remained deserted, and Marimonda in vain scaled the trees and hills in the neighborhood to recover traces of her master.

What had become of him?

CHAPTER IX.

The Precipice.—A Dungeon in a Desert Island.—Resignation.—The passing Bird.—The browsing Goat.—The bending Tree.—Attempts at Deliverance. —Success.—Death of Marimonda.

In that sterile and mountainous quarter of the island to which he has given the name of Stradling,—that name, importing to him misfortune,—Selkirk, venturing in pursuit of a goat, has fallen from a precipice.

Fortunately the cavity is not deep. After a transient swoon, recovering his footing, experiencing only a general numbness, and some pain caused by the contusions resulting from his fall, he bethinks himself of the means of escape.

But a circle of sharp rocks, contracting from the base to the summit, forms a tunnel over his head; no crevice, no precipitous ledge, interrupts their fatal uniformity. Only around him some platforms of sandy earth appear; he digs them with his knife, to form steps. Some fragments of roots project here and there through the interstices of the stones; he hopes to find a point of support by which to scale these abrupt walls. The little solidity of the roots, which give way in his grasp; his sufferings, which become more intense at every effort; these thousand rocky heads bending at once over him; all tell him plainly that it will be impossible for him to emerge from this hole—that it is destined to be his tomb.

Poor young sailor, already condemned to isolation, separated from the rest of mankind, could he have foreseen that one day his captivity was to be still closer! that his steps would be chained, that the sight even of his island would be interdicted! and that in this desert, where he had neither persecutor nor jailer to fear, he would find a prison, a dungeon!

After three days of anguish and tortures, after new and ineffectual attempts,—exhausted by fatigue, by thirst, by hunger,—consumed by fever, supervened in consequence of all his sufferings of body and soul, he resigns himself to his fate; with his foot, he prepares his last couch, composed of sand and dried leaves shaken from above by the neighboring trees; he lies down, folds his arms, closes his eyes, and prepares to die, thinking of his eternal salvation.

Although he tries not to allow himself to be distracted by other thoughts, from time to time sounds from the outer world disturb his pious meditations. First it is the joyous song of a bird. To these vibrating notes another song replies from afar, on a more simple and almost plaintive key. It is doubtless the female, who, with a sort of modest and repressed tenderness, thus announces her retreat to him who calls; then a rapid rustling is heard above the head of the prisoner. It is the songster, hastening to rejoin his companion.

Selkirk has never known love. Once perhaps,—in a fit of youth and delirium; and it was this false love which tore him from his studies, from his country!

Ah! why did he not remain at Largo, with his father? To-day he also would have had a companion! In that smiling country where coolness dwells, where labor is so easy, life so sweet and calm, the paternal roof would have sheltered his happiness! Oh! the joys of his infancy! his green and sunny Scotland.

The regrets which arise in his heart he quickly banishes; his dear remembrances he sacrifices to God; he weaves them into a fervent prayer.

Very soon an approaching bleating rouses him again from his abstractions. A goat, with restless eye, has just stretched her head over the edge of the precipice, and for an instant fixes on him her astonished glance. Then, as if re-assured, defying his powerlessness, with a disdainful lip she quietly crops some tufts of grass growing on the verge of the tunnel.

On seeing her, Selkirk instinctively lays his hand on the lasso which is beside him.

'If I succeed in reaching her, in catching her,' said he, 'her blood will quench the thirst which devours me, her flesh will appease my hunger. But of what use would it be? Whence can I expect aid and succor for my deliverance? This would then only prolong my sufferings.'

And, throwing aside the end of the lasso which he has just seized, he again folds his arms on his breast, and closes his eyes once more.

I know not what stoical philosopher—Atticus, I believe, a prey to a malady which he thought incurable,—had resolved to die of inanition. At the expiration of a certain number of days, abstinence had cured him, and when his friends, in the number of whom he reckoned Cicero, exhorted him to take nourishment, persisting in his first resolution, 'Of what use is it!' said he also, 'Must I not die sooner or later? Why should I then retrace my steps, when I have already travelled more than half the road?'

Selkirk had more reason than Atticus to decide thus; besides, his friends, where are they, to exhort him to live? Friends!—has he ever had any?

Night comes, and with the night a terrific hurricane arises. By the glare of the lightning he sees a tree, situated not far from the tunnel, bend towards him, almost broken by the violence of the wind.

'Perhaps Providence will send me a method of saving myself!' murmured Selkirk; 'should the tree fall on this side, if its branches do not crush me, they will serve as steps to aid me to leave this pit! I am saved!'

But the tree resists the storm, which passes away, carrying with it the last hope of the captive.

Towards the morning of the fourth day his fever has ceased; the tortures of hunger and thirst are no longer felt; the complete annihilation of his strength is to him a kind of relief; sleep seizes him, and with sleep he thinks death must come.

Soon, in his dream, in a hallucination springing undoubtedly from the weakness of his brain, plaints, confused and distant groans, reach him from different points of the island. These sorrowful cries, almost uninterrupted, afterwards approach, and are repeated with increasing strength. He awakes, he listens; the bushes around him crackle and rustle; even the earth emits a dull sound, as beneath the bounding of a goat; the cries are renewed and become more and more distinct, like the sobs of a child. Selkirk puts his hand to his forehead. These plaints, these sobs, he thinks he recognizes, and, suddenly raising himself with a convulsive effort, he exclaims:

'Marimonda!'

And Marimonda runs at her master's voice, changes, on seeing him, her cries of distress for cries of joy, leaps and gambols on the edge of the cavity, and, quickly finding a way to join him, suspends herself by her tail to one of the branches on the verge, and springs to his side.

Then contortions, caresses, winks of the eyes, motions of the head, whining, whistling, succeed each other; she rolls before him, embraces him closely, seeking by every method to supply the place of that speech which alone is wanting, and which she almost seems to have. Good Marimonda! her humid and shivering skin, her bruised and bleeding feet, her in-flamed eyes, plainly tell Selkirk how long she has been in search of him, how she has watched, run, to find him, and, not finding him, what she has suffered at his absence.

Her first transports over, by his pale complexion, by his dim eye, she quickly divines that it is want of food which has reduced him to this condition. Swift as a bird she climbs the sides of the tunnel; she repeatedly goes and returns, bringing each time fruits and canes full of savory and refreshing liquid. It is precisely the usual hour for their first repast, and once more they can partake of it together.

Revived by this repast, by the sight of his companion in exile, Selkirk recovers his ideas of life and liberty. This abyss, from which she ascends with so much facility, who knows but with her aid he may be able in his turn to leave it? He remembers his lasso; he puts one end of it into Marimonda's hand. It is now necessary that she should fix it to some projection of the rock, some strong shrub, which may serve as a point of support.

It was perhaps presuming too much on the intelligence which nature has bestowed on the race of monkeys. At her master's orders, Marimonda would seize the end of the cord, then immediately abandon it, as she needed entire freedom of motion to enable her to scale the walls of the tunnel.

After several ineffectual attempts, Selkirk, as a last resort, decided to encircle Marimonda with the noose of the lasso, and, by a gesture, to send her towards those heights where he was so impatient to join her.

She departs, dragging after her the chain, of which he holds the other extremity: this chain, the only bridge thrown for him between the abyss and the port of safety, between life and death!

With what anxiety he observes, studies its oscillations! Several times he draws it towards him, and each time, as if in reply to his summons, Marimonda suddenly re-appears at the brow of the precipice, preparing to re-descend; but he repulses her with his voice and gestures, and when these methods are insufficient,—when Marimonda, exhausted with lassitude, seated on the verge of the tunnel, persists in remaining motionless, he has recourse to projectiles. To compel her to second him in his work, the possible realization of which he himself scarcely comprehends, he throws at her some fragments of stone detached from his rocky wall, and even the remains of that repast for which he is indebted to her. Even when she is at a distance, informed by the movements of the lasso of the direction she has taken, he pursues her still.

Suddenly the cord tightens in his hand. He pulls again, he pulls with force; the cord resists! Fire mounts to his brain; his sluggish blood is quickened; his heart and temples beat violently; his fever returns, but only to restore to him, at this decisive moment, his former vigor. He hastily digs new steps in the interstices of the rock; with his hands suspending himself to the lasso, assisted by his feet, by his knees, sometimes turning, grasping the projecting roots, the angles of his wall, he at last reaches the top of the cliff.

Suddenly he feels the lasso stretch, as if about to break; a mist passes over his eyes: his head becomes dizzy, the cord escapes his grasp. But, by a mechanical movement, he has seized one of the highest projections of the tunnel, he holds it, he climbs,—he is saved.

And during this perilous ascension, absorbed in the difficulties of the undertaking, attentive to himself alone, staggering, with a buzzing sound in his ears, he has not heard a sorrowful, lamentable moaning, not far from him.

Dragging hither and thither after her the rope of leather and fibre of aloes, Marimonda, rather, doubtless, by chance than by calculation, had enlaced it around the trunk of the same tree which the night before, during the storm, had agitated its dishevelled branches above the deep couch of the dying man. This trunk had served as a point of resistance; but, during the tension, the unfortunate monkey, with her breast against the tree, had herself been caught in the folds of the lasso.

When Selkirk arrives, he finds her extended on the ground, blood and foam issuing from her mouth, and her eyes starting from their sockets. Kneeling beside her, he loosens the bonds which still detain her. Excited by his presence, Marimonda makes an effort to rise, but immediately falls back, uttering a new cry of pain.

With his heart full of anguish, taking her in his arms, Selkirk, not without a painful effort, not without being obliged to pause on the way to recover his strength, carries her to the dwelling on the shore.

This shore he finds deserted and in confusion.

Deprived of their daily nourishment during the prolonged absence of their master, the goats have made a passage through the inclosure, by gnawing the still green foliage which imprisoned them; the hurricane of the night has overthrown the rest. Before leaving, they had ravaged the garden, destroyed the promises of the approaching harvest, and devoured even the bark of the young trees. The cats have followed the goats. Selkirk has before his eyes a spectacle of desolation; his props, his trellises, the remains of his orchard, of his inclosure, of his shed, a part even of the roof of his cabin, strew the earth in confusion around him.

But it is not this which occupies him now. He has prepared for Marimonda a bed beside his own; he takes care of her, he watches over her, he leaves her only to seek in the woods, or on the mountains, the herb which may heal her; he brings all sorts, and by armfuls, that she may choose;—does she not know them better than himself?

As she turns away her head, or repulses with the hand those which he presents, he thinks he has not yet discovered the one she requires, and though still suffering, though himself exhausted by so many varying emotions, he recommences his search, to summon the entire island to the assistance of Marimonda. From each of his trees he borrows a branch; from his bushes, his rocks, his streams—a plant, a fruit, a leaf, a root! For the first time he ventures across the *pajonals*—spongy marshes formed by the sea along the cliffs, and where, beneath the shade of the mangroves, grow those singular vegetables, those gelatinous plants, endowed with vitality and motion. At sight of all these remedies, Marimonda closes her eyes, and reopens them only to address to her friend a look of gratitude.

The only thing she accepts is the water he offers her, the water which he himself holds to her lips in his cocoa-nut cup.

During a whole week, Selkirk remains constantly absorbed in these cares, useless cares!—Marimonda cannot be healed! In her breast, bruised by the folds of the lasso, exists an important lesion of the organs essential to life, and from time to time a gush of blood reddens her white teeth.

'What!' said Selkirk to himself, 'she has then accompanied me on this corner of earth only to be my victim! To her first caress I replied only by brutality; the first shot I fired in this island was directed against her. I pursued for a long time, with my thoughtless and stupid hatred, the only being who has ever loved me, and who to-day is dying for having saved me from that precipice from which I drove her with blows of stones! Marimonda, my companion, my friend,—no! thou shalt not die! He who sent thee to me as a consolation will not take thee away so soon, to leave me a thousand times more alone, more unhappy, than ever! God, in clothing thee with a form almost human, has undoubtedly given thee a soul almost like ours; the gleam of tenderness and intelligence which shines in thine eyes, where could it have been lighted, but at that divine fire whence all affection and devotion emanate? Well! I will implore Him for thee; and if He refuse to hear me, it will be because He has forgotten me, because He has entirely forsaken me, and I shall have nothing more to expect from His mercy!'

Falling then upon his knees, with his forehead upon the ground, he prays God for Marimonda.

Meanwhile, from day to day the poor invalid grows weaker; her eyes become dim and glassy; her limbs frightfully emaciated, and her hair comes off in large masses.

One evening, exhausted with fatigue, after having wrapped in a covering of goat-skin Marimonda, who was in a violent fever, Selkirk was preparing to retire to rest; she detained him, and, taking his hand in both of hers, cast upon him a gentle and prolonged look, which resembled an adieu.

He seated himself beside her on the ground.

Then, without letting go his hand, she leaned her head on her master's knee, and fell asleep in this position. Selkirk dares not stir, for fear of disturbing her repose. Insensibly sleep seizes him also.

In the morning when he awakes, the sun is illuminating the interior of his cabin; Marimonda remains in the same attitude as the evening before, but her hands are cold, and a swarm of flies and mosquitoes are thrusting their sharp trunks into her eyes and ears.

She is a corpse.

Selkirk raises her, uttering a cry, and, after having cast an angry look towards heaven, wipes away two tears that trickle down his cheeks.

Thou thoughtest thyself insensible, Selkirk, and behold, thou art weeping!—thou, who hast more than once seen, with unmoistened eye, men, thy companions, in war or at sea, fall beneath a furious sword, or under the fire of batteries! Among the sentiments which honor humanity, which elevate it notwithstanding its defects, thou hadst preserved at least thy confidence in God and in his mercy, Selkirk, and to-day thou doubtest both!

Why dost thou weep? why dost thou distrust God?

Because thy monkey is dead!

CHAPTER X.

Discouragement.—A Discovery.—A Retrospective Glance.—Project of Suicide.—The Last Shot.—The Sea Serpent.—The *Porro*.—A Message. —Another Solitary.

His provisions are exhausted, and Selkirk thinks not of renewing them; his settlement on the shore is destroyed, and he thinks not of rebuilding it; the fish-pond, the bed of water-cresses are encroached upon by sand and weeds, and he thinks not of repairing them. His mind, completely discouraged, recoils before such labors; he has scarcely troubled himself to replace the roof of his cabin.

In the midst of his dreams, Selkirk had not counted enough on two terrific guests, which must sooner or later come: despair and *ennui*.

Nevertheless, he had read in his Bible this passage: 'As the worm gnaweth the garment and rottenness the wood, so doth the weariness of solitude gnaw the heart of man.'

One day, as he was descending from the Oasis, where he had dug a tomb for Marimonda, he bethought himself of visiting the site of his burning wood.

Around him, the earth, blackened by the ravages of the fire, presented only a naked, gloomy and desolate picture. To his great surprise, beneath the ruins, under coal dust and half-calcined trunks of trees, he discovered, elevated several feet above the soil, the partition of a wall, some stones quarried out and placed one upon another; in fine, the remains of a building, evidently constructed by the hand of man.

Men had then inhabited this island before him! What had become of them? This wood, impenetrably choked, stifled with thorny bushes, briars and vines, and which he had delivered over to the flames, was undoubtedly a garden planted by them, on a sheltered declivity of the mountain; the garden which surrounded their habitation, as he had himself designed his own to do.

Ah! if he could have but found them in the island, how different would have been his fate! But to live alone! to have no companions but his own thoughts!

amid the dash of waves, the cry of birds, the bleating of goats, incessantly to imagine the sound of a human voice, and incessantly to experience the torture of being undeceived! What elements of happiness has he ever met in this miserable island? When he dreamed of creating resources for a long and peaceful future, he lied to himself. A life favored by leisure would but crush him the oftener beneath the weight of thought, and it is thought which is killing him, the thought of isolation!

What import to him the beautiful sights spread out before his eyes? The vast extent of sky and earth has repeated to him each day that he is lost, forgotten on an obscure point of the globe. The sunrises and sunsets, with their magic aspects, this luxuriant tropical vegetation, the magnificent and picturesque scenery of his island, awaken in him only a feeling of restraint, an uneasiness which he cannot define. Perhaps the emotions, so sweet to all, are painful to him only because he cannot communicate them, share them with another. It is not the noisy life of cities which he asks, not even that of the shore. But, at least, a companion, a being to reply to his voice, to be associated with his joys, his sorrows. Marimonda! No, he recognizes it now! Marimonda could amuse him, but was not sufficient; she inhabited with him only the exterior world, she communicated with him only by things visible and palpable; her affection for her master, her gentleness, her admirable instinct, sometimes succeeded in lessening the distance which separated their two natures, but did not wholly fill up the interval.

He had exaggerated the intelligence which, besides, increased at the expense of her strength, as with all monkeys; for God has not willed that an animal should approximate too closely to man; he had overrated the sense of her acts, because he needed near him a thinking and acting being; but with her, confidences, plans, hopes, communication, the exchange of all those intimate and mysterious thoughts which are the life of the soul, were they possible? Even her eyes did not see like his own; admiration was forbidden to her; admiration, that precious faculty, which exists only for man,—and which becomes extinct by isolation.

How many others become extinct also!

Self-love, a just self-esteem, that powerful lever which sustains us, which elevates us, which compels us to respect in ourselves that nobility of race which we derive from God, what becomes of it in solitude? For Selkirk, vanity itself has lost its power to stimulate. Formerly, when in the presence of his comrades at St. Andrew or of the royal fleet, he had signalized himself by feats of address or courage, a sentiment of pride or triumph had inspired him. Since his arrival in the island, his courage and address have had but too frequent opportunities of exercising themselves, but he has been excited only by want, by necessity, by a purely personal interest. Besides, can one utter an exclamation of triumph, where there is not even an echo to repeat it?

After having thus painfully passed in review all of which his exile from the world had deprived him, he exclaimed:

'To live alone, what a martyrdom! to live useless to all, what a disgrace! What! does no one need me? What! are generosity, devotion, even pity, all those noble instincts by which the soul reveals itself, for ever interdicted to me? This is death, death premature and shameful! Ah! why did I not remain at the foot of that precipice?'

With downcast head, he remained some time overwhelmed with the weight of his discouragement; then, suddenly, his brow cleared up, a sinister thought crossed his mind; he ran to his cabin, seized his gun. This last shot, this last charge of powder and lead, which he has preserved so preciously as a final resource, it will serve to put an end to his days! Well, is not this the most valuable service he can expect from it? He examines the gun; the priming is yet undisturbed; he passes his nail over the flint, leans the butt against the ground, takes off the thick leather which covers his foot, that he may be able to fire with more certainty. But during all these preparations his resolution grows weaker; he trembles as he rests the gun against his temples; that sentiment of self-preservation, so profoundly implanted in the heart of man, re-awakens in him. He hesitates—thrice returning to his first resolution, he brings the gun to his forehead; thrice he removes it. At last, to drive away this demon of suicide, he fires it in the air.

Scarcely has he thus uselessly thrown away this precious shot before he repents. He approaches the shore; it is at the moment when the tide is at its lowest ebb; the sun touches the horizon. Selkirk lies down on the damp beach: —'When the wave returns,' said he, 'if it be God's will, let it take me!'

Slumber comes first. Exhausted with emotion, yielding to the lassitude of his mind, he falls asleep. In the middle of the night, suddenly awakened by the sound of the advancing wave, he again flees before the threat of death; he no longer wishes to die. Once in safety, he turns to contemplate that immense sea which, for an instant, he had wished might be his tomb.

By the moonlight, he perceives as it were a long and slender chain, which, gliding upon the crest of the waves, directs itself towards the shore. By its form, by its copper color, by the multiplicity of its rings, unfolding in the distance, Selkirk recognizes the sea-serpent, that terror of navigators, as he has often heard it described.

The mind of the solitary is a perpetual mirage.

Filled with terror, he flies again; he conceals himself, trembling, in the caverns of his mountains; he has become a coward; why should he affect a courage he does not feel? No one is looking at him!

The next day, instead of the sea-serpent, he finds on the beach an immense cryptogamia, a gigantic alga, of a single piece, divided into a thousand cylindrical branches, and much superior to all those he has observed in the Straits of Sunda. The rising tide had thrown it on the shore.

While he examines it, he sees with surprise all sorts of birds come to peck at it; coatis, agoutis, and even rats, come out of their holes, boldly carrying away before his eyes fragments, whence issues a thick and brown sap. Emboldened by their example, and especially by the balsamic odor of the plant, he tastes it. It is sweet and succulent.

This plant is no other than that providential vegetable called by the Spaniards *porro*, and which forms so large a part of the nourishment of the poor inhabitants of Chili.[1]

[1]

> It is the *Durvilloea utilis*, dedicated to Dumont d'Urville, by Bory de St. Vincent, and classed by him in the laminariées, an important and valuable family of marine cryptogamia.

The sea, which had already sent Selkirk seals to furnish him with oil and furs in a moment of distress, had just come to his assistance by giving him an easily procured aliment for a long time.

Another surprise awaits him.

Between the interlaced branches of his alga, he discovers a little bottle, strongly secured with a cork and wax. It contains a fragment of parchment, on which are traced some lines in the Spanish language.

Although he is but imperfectly acquainted with this language, though the characters are partially effaced or scarcely legible, Selkirk, by dint of patience and study, soon deciphers the following words:

'In the name of the Holy Trinity, to you who may read'—(here some words were wanting,)—'greeting. My name is Jean Gons—(Gonzalve or Gonsales; the rest of the name was illegible.) After having seen my two sons, and almost all my fortune, swallowed up in the sea with the vessel *Fernand Cortes*, in which I was a passenger, thrown by shipwreck on the coasts of the Island of San Ambrosio, near Chili, I live here alone and desolate. May God and men come to my aid!'

At the bottom of the parchment, some other characters were perceptible, but without form, without connection, and almost entirely destroyed by a slight mould which had collected at the bottom of the bottle.

CHAPTER XI.

The Island San Ambrosio.—Selkirk at last knows what Friendship is.—The Raft.—Visits to the Tomb of Marimonda.—The Departure.—The two Islands.—Shipwreck.—The Port of Safety.

As he read this, Selkirk was seized with intense pity for the unfortunate shipwrecked. What! on this same ocean, undoubtedly on these same shores, lives another unhappy being, like himself exiled from the world, enduring the same sufferings, subject to the same wants, experiencing the same *ennui*, the same anguish as himself! this man has confided to the sea his cry of distress, his complaint, and the sea, a faithful messenger, has just deposited it at the feet of Selkirk!

Suddenly he remembers that rock, that island, discerned by him, on the day when at the Oasis, he was reconciled to Marimonda.

That is the island of San Ambrosio; it is there, he does not doubt it for an instant, that his new friend lives; yes, his friend! for, from this moment he experiences for him an emotion of sympathetic affection. He loves him, he is so much to be pitied! Poor father, he has lost his sons, he has lost his fortune and the hope of returning to his country; and yet there reigns in his letter a tone of dignified calmness, of religious resignation which can come only from a noble heart. He is a Spaniard and a Roman Catholic; Selkirk is a Scotchman and a Presbyterian; what matters it?

To-day his friend demands assistance, and he has resolved to dare all, to undertake all to respond to his appeal. Like a lamp deprived of air, his mind has revived at this idea, that he can at last be useful to others than himself. The inhabitant of San Ambrosio shall be indebted to him for an alleviation of his sorrows; for companionship in them. What is there visionary about this hope? Had he not already conceived the project of preparing a barque to explore that unknown coast? God seems to encourage his design, by sending him at once this double manna for the body and soul, the *porro*, which will suffice for his nourishment, and this writing, which the wave has just brought, to impose on him a duty.

He immediately sets himself to the work, and obstacles are powerless to chill his generous excitement. Of the vegetable productions of the island, the red cedar and myrtle are those which grow of the largest size;[1] but yet their trunks are not large enough to serve when hollowed out for a barque. Well! he will construct a raft.

[1]

The *myrtus maximus* attains 13 metres (a little more than 42 feet) in height.]

He fells young trees, cuts off their branches, rolls them to the shore, on a platform of sand, which the waves reach at certain periods; he fastens them solidly together with a triple net-work of plaited leather, cords woven of the fibre of the aloe, supple and tough vines; he chooses another with diverging and horizontal roots, the habitual direction taken by all the large vegetables of this island, the sand of which is covered only by two feet of earth. This shall be the mast. He plants it in the middle of the raft, where it is kept upright by its roots, knotted and interwoven with the various pieces which compose the floor. For a sail, has he not that which was left him by the Swordfish? and will not his seal-skin hammock serve as a spare sail?

He afterwards constructs a helm, then two strong oars, that he may neglect no chance of success. He fastens his structure still more firmly by all that remains to him of his nails and bolts, and awaits the high tide to launch his skiff upon the sea.

He has never felt calmer, happier, than during the long time occupied in these labors; their object has doubled his strength. The moments of indispensable repose, he has passed at the Oasis, beside the tomb of Marimonda, of that Marimonda, who by her example, opened to him the life of devotedness in which he has just engaged. Thence, with his eye turned upon that island where dwells the unknown friend from whom he has received a summons, he talks to him, encourages him, consoles him; he imparts to him his resolution to join him soon, and it seems as if the same waves which had brought the message will also undertake to transmit the reply.

At present, Selkirk finds some sweetness in pitying evils which are not his own; he no longer dreams of wrapping himself in a cloak of selfishness; that disdainful heart, hitherto invincibly closed, at last experiences friendship, or at least aspires to do so.

At last, the day arrives when the sea, inundating the marshes, bending the mangroves, reaches, on the sandy platform, one of the corners of his raft.

Selkirk hastens to transport thither his hatchets, his guns, his seal-skins and goat-skins, his Bible, his spy-glass, his pipes, his ladder, his stools, even his traps; all his riches! it is a complete removal.

On taking possession of the island, he had engraved on the bark of several trees the date of his arrival; he now inscribes upon them the day of his departure. For many months his reckoning has been interrupted; to determine the date is impossible; he knows only the day of the week.

When the wave had entirely raised his barque, aiding himself with one of the long oars to propel it over the rocky bottom, he gained the sea. Then, after having adjusted his sail, with his hand on the helm, he turned towards his island to address to it an adieu, laden with maledictions rather than regrets.

Swelled by a south-east wind, the sail pursues its course towards that other land, the object of his new desires. At the expiration of some hours, by the aid of his glass, what from the summit of his mountains had appeared to him only a dark point, a rock beaten by the waves, seems already enlarged, allowing him to see high hills covered with verdure. He has not then deceived himself! There exists a habitable land,—habitable for two! It has served as a refuge to the shipwrecked man, to his friend! Ah! how impatient he is to reach this shore where he is to meet him!

Several hours more of a slow but peaceful navigation roll away. He has arrived at a distance almost midway between the point of departure and that of arrival. Looking alternately at the islands Selkirk and San Ambrosio, both illuminated by the sunset, with their indefinite forms, their bases buried in the waves, their terraced summits, veiled with a light fog, they appear like the reflection of each other. But for the discovery which he had previously made of the second, he would have believed this was his own island, or rather its image, represented in the waters of the sea.

But in proportion as he advances towards his new conquest, it increases to his eyes, as if to testify the reality of its existence, now by a mountain peak, now by a cape. He had seen only the profile, it now presents its face, ready to develope all its graces, all its fascinations; while its rival, disdained, abandoned, becomes by degrees effaced, and seems to wish to conceal its humiliation beneath the wave of the great ocean.

Suddenly, without any apparent jar, without any flaw of wind, on a calm sea, the stem of the tree serving as a mast vacillates, bends forward, then on one side; the roots, which fasten it to the floor of the raft, are wrenched from their hold; the sail, diverging in the same direction, still extended, drags it entirely down, and it is borne away by the wave.

Struck with astonishment, Selkirk puts his foot on the helm, and seizes his oars; but oars are powerless to move so heavy a machine. What is to be done?

He who has not been able to endure isolation in the midst of a terrestrial paradise, from which he has just voluntarily exiled himself, must he then he reduced to have for an asylum, on the immensity of the ocean, only a few trunks of trees scarcely lashed together?

The situation is frightful, terrific; Selkirk dares not contemplate it, lest his reason should give way. He must have a sail; a mast! He has his spare sail; for the mast, his only resource is to detach one of the timbers which compose the frame-work of his raft. Perhaps this will destroy its solidity; but he has no choice.

He takes the best of his hatchets, chooses among the straight stems of which his floating dwelling is composed, that which seems most suitable; he cuts away with a thousand precautions, the bonds which fasten it; he frees it, not without difficulty, from the contact of other logs to which it has been attached. But while he devotes himself to this task, the raft, obedient to a mysterious motion of the sea, has slowly drifted on; the surface is covered with foam, as if sub-marine waves are lashing it. Selkirk springs to the helm; the tiller breaks in his hands; he seizes the oars, they also break. An unknown force hurries him on. He has just fallen into one of those rapid currents which, from north to south, traverse the waters of the Pacific Ocean.

Borne away in a contrary direction from that which he has hitherto pursued, the land of which he had come in search seems to fly before him. Whither is he going? Into what regions, into what solitudes of the sea is he to be carried, far from islands and continents?

To add to his terror, in these latitudes, where day suddenly succeeds to night and night to day, where twilight is unknown, the sun, just now shining brightly, suddenly sinks below the horizon.

In the midst of profound darkness, the unhappy man pursues this fatal race, leading to inevitable destruction. During a part of this terrible night, he hears the frail frame-work which supports him cracking beneath his feet. How long must his sufferings last? He knows not. At last, jostled by adverse waves, shaken to its centre, the raft begins to whirl around, and something heavier than the shock of the wave comes repeatedly to give it new and rude blows. The first rays of the rising moon, far from calming the terrors of the unhappy mariner, increase them. In his dizzy brain, these wan rays which silver the surface of the sea, seem so many phantoms coming to be present at his last moments. Pale, bent double, with his hair standing upright, clinging to some projection of his barque, he in vain attempts to fix his glance on certain strange objects which he sees ascending, descending, and rolling around him.

They are the trunks of the trees which formed a part of his raft, limbs detached from its body, and which, now drawn into the same whirlpool, are by their repeated shocks, aiding in his complete destruction.

In face of this imminent, implacable death, Selkirk ceases to struggle against it. He has now but one resource; the belief in another life. The religious instinct, which has already come to his assistance, revives with force. Clinging with his hands and feet to these wavering timbers, which are almost disjoined, half inundated by the wave, which is encroaching more and more upon his last asylum, he directs his steps towards the spot where he had deposited his arms and furs; he takes from among them his Bible, not to read it, but to clasp it to his heart, whose agitation and terror seem to grow calm beneath its sacred contact.

He then attempts to absorb his thoughts in God; he blames himself for not having been contented with the gifts he had received from Him; he might have lived happily in Scotland, or in the royal navy. It is this perpetual desire for change, these aspirations after the unknown, which have occasioned his ruin.

At this moment, raising his eyes towards heaven, he sees, beneath the pale rays of the moon, a mass of rocks rising at a little distance, which he immediately recognizes. There is the bay of the Seals, the peak of the Discovery. That hollow, lying in the shadow, is the valley of the Oasis! As on the first day of his arrival, on one of the steepest summits of the mountain, he perceives stationed there, immovable, like a sentinel, a goat, between whose delicate limbs shines a group of stars, celestial eyes, whose golden lids seem to vibrate as if in appeal. It is his island! He does not hesitate; suddenly recovering all his energies, he springs from the raft, struggles with vigor, with perseverance against the current, triumphs over it, and, after prolonged efforts, at last reaches this haven of deliverance, this port of safety; he lands, fatigued, exhausted, but overcome with joy and gratitude. Profoundly thanking God from his heart, he prostrates himself, and kisses with transport the hospitable soil of this island,—which, on the morning of the same day, he had cursed.

Alas! does not reflection quickly diminish this lively joy at his return and safety? From this shipwreck, poor sailor, thou hast saved only thyself: thy tools, thy instruments of labor, even thy Bible, are a prey to the sea!

It is now, Selkirk, that thou must suffice for thyself! It is the last trial to which thou canst be subjected!

CHAPTER XII.

The Island of Juan Fernandez.—Encounter in the Mountains.—Discussion. —A New Captivity.—A Cannon-shot.—Dampier and Selkirk.—*Mas a Fuera*. —News of Stradling.—Confidences.—End of the History of the real Robinson Crusoe.—Nebuchadnezzar.

On the 1st of February, 1709, an English vessel, equipped and sent to sea by the merchants of Bristol, after having sailed around Cape Horn, in company with another vessel belonging to the same expedition, touched alone, about the 33d degree of south latitude, at the Island of Juan Fernandez, from a hundred and ten to a hundred and twenty leagues distant from the coast of Chili.

The second ship was to join her without delay. Symptoms of the scurvy had appeared on board, and it was intended to remain here for some time, to give the crew opportunity of recovering their health.

Their tents pitched, towards evening several sailors, having ventured upon the island, were not a little surprised to see, through the obscurity, a strange being, bearing some resemblance to the human form, who, at their approach, scaling the mountains, leaping from rock to rock, fled with the rapidity of a deer, the lightness of a chamois.

Some doubted whether it was a man, and prepared to fire at him. They were prevented by an officer named Dower, who accompanied them.

On their return to their companions, the sailors related what they had seen; Dower did not fail to do the same among the officers; and this evening, at the encampment on the shore, in the forecastle as well as on the quarter-deck, there were narratives and suppositions that would 'amuse an assembly of Puritans through the whole of Lent,' says the account from which we borrow a part of our information.

At this period, tales of the marvellous gained great credence among sailors. Not long before, the Spaniards had discovered giants in Patagonia; the Portuguese, sirens in the seas of Brazil; the French, tritons and satyrs at Martinique; the Dutch, black men, with feet like lobsters, beyond Paramaribo.

The strange individual under discussion was unquestionably a satyr, or at least one of those four-footed, hairy men, such as the authentic James Carter declared he had met with in the northern part of America.

Some, thinking this conclusion too simple, adroitly insinuated that no one among the sailors who had met this monster, had noticed in him so great a number of paws. Why four paws?—why should he not be a monopedous man, a man whose body, terminated by a single leg, cleared, with this support alone, considerable distances? Was not the existence of the monopedous man attested by modern travellers, and even in antiquity and the middle ages, by Pliny and St. Augustine?

Others preferred to imagine in this singular personage the acephalous man, the man without a head, named by the grave Baumgarthen as existing on the new continent. They had not discovered many legs, but neither had they discovered a head; why should he have one?

And the discussion continued, and not a voice was raised to risk this judicious observation; if neither head nor limbs have been distinguished, it may perhaps be because he has been seen only in the dark.

The next day, each wished to be satisfied; a regular hunt was organized against this phenomenon; they set out, invaded his retreat, pursued him, surrounded him, at last seized him, and the brave sailors of Great Britain discovered with stupefaction, in this monopedous, acephalous man, in this satyr, this cercopithecus, what? A countryman, a Scotchman, a subject of Queen Anne!

It was Selkirk; Selkirk, his hair long and in disorder, his limbs encased in fragments of skins, and half deprived of his reason.

His island was Juan Fernandez, so called by the first navigator who discovered it; this was Selkirk Island.

When he was conducted before Captain Woodes Rogers, commander of the expedition, to the interrogations of the latter, the unfortunate man, with downcast look, and agitated with a nervous trembling, replied only by repeating mechanically the last syllables of the phrases which were addressed to him by the captain.

A little recovered from his agitation, discovering that he had Englishmen to deal with, he attempted to pronounce some words; he could only mutter a few incoherent and disconnected sentences.

'Solitude and the care of providing for his subsistence,' says Paw, 'had so occupied his mind, that all rational ideas were effaced from it. As savage as the animals, and perhaps more so, he had almost entirely forgotten the secret of articulating intelligible sounds.'

Captain Rogers having asked him how long he had been secluded in this island, Selkirk remained silent; he nevertheless understood the question, for his eyes immediately opened with terror, as if he had just measured the long space of time which his exile had lasted. He was far from having an exact idea of it; he appreciated it only by the sufferings he had endured there, and, looking fixedly at his hands, he opened and shut them several times.

Reckoning by the number of his fingers, it was twenty or thirty years, and every one at first believed in the accuracy of his calculation, so completely did his forehead, furrowed with wrinkles, his skin blackened, withered by the sun, his hair whitened at the roots, his gray beard, give him the aspect of an old man.

Selkirk was born in 1680; he was then only twenty-nine.

After having replied thus, he turned his head, cast a troubled look on the objects which surrounded him; a remembrance seemed to awaken, and, uttering a cry, stepping forward, he pointed with his finger to a cedar on his left. It was the tree on which, when he left the Swordfish, he had inscribed the date of his arrival in the island. The officer Dower approached, and, notwithstanding the crumbling of the decayed bark, could still read there this inscription:

'Alexander Selkirk—from Largo, Scotland, Oct. 27, 1704.'

His exile from the world had therefore lasted four years and three months.

Notwithstanding the interest excited by his misfortunes, by his name, his accent, more than by his language, Captain Rogers, an honorable and humane man, but of extreme severity on all that appertained to discipline, recognized him as a British subject, suspected him to be a deserter from the English navy, and gave orders that he should be put under guard, pending a definitive decision.

The sailors commissioned to this office did not find it an easy thing to guard a prisoner who could climb the trees like a squirrel, and outstrip them all in a race. As a precaution, they commenced by binding him firmly to the same cedar on which his name was engraved. There the unfortunate Selkirk figured as a curious animal, ornamented with a label.

Afterwards, more for pastime than through mischief, they tormented him with questions, to obtain from him hesitating or almost senseless replies, which bewildered him much; then they began to examine, with childish surprise, the length of his beard, of his hair and nails; the prodigious development of his muscles; his bare feet, so hardened by travel, that they seemed to be covered with horn moccasins. Having found beneath his goat-skin rags, a knife, whose blade, by dint of use and sharpening, was almost reduced to the proportions of that of a penknife, they took it away to examine it; but on seeing himself deprived of this single weapon, the only relic of his shipwreck, the prisoner struggled, uttering wild howls; they restored it to him.

At the hour of repast, Selkirk had, like the rest, his portion of meat and biscuit. He ate the biscuit, manifesting great satisfaction; but he, who had at first suffered so much from being deprived of salt, found in the meat a degree of saltness insupportable. He pointed to the stream; one of his guards courteously offered him his gourd, containing a mixture of rum and water; he approached it to his lips, and immediately threw it away with violence, as if it had burned him.

At evening, he was transported on board.

A few days after he began to acquire a taste for common food; his ideas became more definite; speech returned to his lips more freely and clearly; but liberty of motion was not yet restored to him, a new captivity opened before him, and his irritation at this was presenting an obstacle to the complete restoration of his faculties, when God, who had so deeply tried him, came to his assistance.

One morning, as the crew of the ship were occupied, some in caulking and tarring it, others in gathering edible plants on the island, a cannon-shot resounded along the waves. The caulkers climbed up the rigging, the provision-hunters ran to the shore, the officers seized their spy-glasses, and all together quickly uttered a *huzza*! The vessel which had sailed in company with that of Captain Rogers, the Duchess, of Bristol, had arrived. This vessel, commanded by William Cook, had, for a master-pilot, a man more celebrated in maritime annals than the commanders of the expedition themselves;—this was Dampier, the indefatigable William Dampier, who, a short time since a millionaire, now completely ruined in consequence of foolish speculations and prodigalities, had just undertaken a third voyage around the world.

Scarcely had he disembarked, when he heard of the great event of the day—of the wild man. His name was mentioned, he remembered having known an Alexander Selkirk at St. Andrew, at the inn of the Royal Salmon. He went to him, interrogated him, recognized him, and, without loss of time, after having had his hair and beard cut, and procured suitable clothing for him, presented him to Capt. Rogers; he introduced him as one of his old comrades, formerly an intrepid and distinguished officer in the navy, one of the conquerors of Vigo, who had been induced by himself to embark in the Swordfish, partly at his expense.

Restored to liberty, supported, revived, by the kind cares of Dampier, his old hero, Selkirk felt rejuvenated. His first thought then is for that other unfortunate man, still an exile perhaps in his desert island. After having informed the old sailor that he had found a little bottle, containing a written parchment, he said: 'Dear Captain, it would be a meritorious act, and one worthy of you, to co-operate in the deliverance of this unhappy man. A boat will suffice for the voyage, since the Island of San Ambrosio is so near this. Oh! how joyfully would I accompany you in this excursion!'

'My brave hermit,' replied Dampier, shaking his head, 'the neighboring island of which you speak is no other than the second in this group, named *Mas a Fuera*. As for the other, that San Ambrosio which you think so near, if it has not become a floating island since my last voyage, if it is still where I left it, under the Tropic of Capricorn, to reach it will not be so trifling a matter; besides, your little bottle must be a bottle of ink. There is here confusion of place and confusion of time; not only is *Mas a Fuera* not *San Ambrosio* but this latter island, far from being a desert, as your correspondent has said, has been inhabited more than twenty years by a multitude of madmen, fishermen and pirates, potato-eaters and old sailors, who, when I visited them, in 1702, politely received me with gun-shots, and whose politeness I returned with cannon-shots. Therefore, my boy, he who wrote to you must have been dead when you received his letter. What date did it bear?'

'None,' said Selkirk; 'the last lines were effaced;' and he trembled at the idea of all the dangers he had run in pursuit of this friend, who no longer existed, and of a land which he had never inhabited.

After having satisfied a duty of humanity, that which he had regarded as a debt contracted towards a friend, Selkirk, among other inquiries, let fall the name of Stradling. This time, it was hatred which askedinformation.

His hatred was destined to be gratified.

In pursuing his voyage, after having coasted along the shores of the Straits of Magellan, Stradling, surprised by a frightful hurricane, had seen his vessel entirely disabled. Repulsed at five different times, now by the tempest, now by the Spaniards, from the ports where he attempted to take refuge, he was thrown, near La Plata, on an inhospitable shore. Attacked, pillaged by the natives, half of his crew having perished, with the remains of his ship he constructed another, to which he gave the name of the Cinque Ports, instead of that of the Swordfish, which it was no longer worthy to bear. This was a large pinnace, on which he had secretly returned to England. For several years past, Dampier had not heard of him.

Selkirk thought himself sufficiently avenged; his present happiness silenced his past ill-will. He even became reconciled to his island.

Each day he traversed its divers parts, with emotions various as the remembrances it awakened. But he was now no longer alone! Arm and arm with Dampier, he revisited these places where he had suffered so much, and which often resumed for him their enchanting aspects.

His companion was soon informed of his history. When he had related what we already know, from his landing to the construction of his raft, and to his frightful shipwreck, he at last commenced, not without some mortification, the recital of his final miseries, which alone could explain the deplorable state in which the English sailors had found him.

By the loss of his hatchets, his ladder, his other instruments of labor, condemned to inaction, to powerlessness, he had nothing to occupy himself with but to provide sustenance. But the sea had taken his snares along with the rest. He at first subsisted on herbs, fruits and roots; afterwards his stomach rejected these crudities, as it had repulsed the fish. Armed with a stick, he had chased the agoutis; for want of agoutis, he had eaten rats.

By night, he silently climbed the trees to surprise the female of the toucan or blackbird, which he pitilessly stifled over their young brood. Meanwhile, at the noise he made among the branches, this winged prey almost always escaped him.

He tried to construct a ladder; by the aid of his knife alone, he attempted to cut down two tall trees. During this operation his knife broke—only a fragment remained. This was for him a great trial.

He thought of making, with reeds and the fibres of the aloe, a net to catch birds; but all patient occupation, all continuous labor, had become insupportable to him.

That he might escape the gloomy ideas which assailed him more and more, it became necessary to avoid repose, to court bodily fatigue.

By continual exercise, his powers of locomotion had developed in incredible proportions. His feet had become so hardened that he no longer felt the briers or sharp stones. When he grew weary, he slept, in whatever place he found himself, and these were his only quiet hours.

To chase the agoutis had ceased to be an object worthy of his efforts; the kids took their turn, afterwards the goats. He had acquired such dexterity of movement, and such strength of muscle, such certainty of eye, that to leap from one projection of rock to another, to spring at one bound over ravines and deep cavities, was to him but a childish sport. In these feats he took pleasure and pride.

Sometimes, in the midst of his flights through space, he would seize a bird on the wing.

The goats themselves soon lost their power to struggle against such a combatant. Notwithstanding their number, had Selkirk wished it, he might have depopulated the island. He was careful not to do this.

If he wished to procure a supply of provisions, he directed his steps towards the most elevated peaks of the mountain, marked his game, pursued it, caught it by the horns, or felled it by a blow from his stick; after which his knife-blade did its office. The goat killed, he threw it on his shoulders, and, almost as swiftly as before, regained the cavernous grotto or leafy tree, in the shelter of which he could this day eat and sleep. He had for a long time forsaken his cabin, which was too far distant from his hunting-grounds.

If he had a stock of provision on hand, he still pursued the goats as usual, but only for his personal gratification. If he caught one, he contented himself with slitting its ear; this was his seal, the mark by which he recognized his free flock. During the last years of his abode in the island, he had killed or marked thus nearly five hundred.[1]

[1]

> Long after his departure from Juan Fernandez, the ship's crews, who came there for supplies, or the pirates who took refuge there, found goats whose ears had been slit by Selkirk's knife.

In the natural course of things, as his physical powers increased, his intelligence became enfeebled.

Necessity had at first aroused his industry, for all industry awakes at the voice of want; but his own had been due rather to his recollections than to his ingenuity. He thought himself a creator, he was only an imitator.

Whatever may have been said by those who, in the pride of a deceitful philosophy, have wished to glorify the power of the solitary man—if the latter, supported by certain fortunate circumstances, can remain some time in a state hardly endurable, it is not by his own strength, but by means which society itself has furnished. This is the incontestable truth, from which, in his pride, Selkirk had turned away.

Deprived of exercise and of aliment, his thoughts, no longer sustained by reading the Holy Book, were day by day lost in a chaos of dreams and reveries.

A prey to terrors which he could not explain, he feared darkness, he trembled at the slightest sound of the wind among the branches; if it blew violently, he thought the trees would be uprooted and crush him; if the sea roared, he trembled at the idea of the submersion of his entire island.

When he traversed the woods, especially if the heat was great, he often heard, distinctly, voices which called him or replied. He caught entire phrases; others remained unfinished. These phrases, connected neither with his thoughts nor his situation, were strange to him. Sometimes he even recognized the voice.

Now it was that of Catherine, scolding her servants; now that of Stradling, of Dampier, or one of his college tutors. Once he heard thus the voice of one of his classmates whom he least remembered; at another time it was that of his old admiral, Rourke, uttering the words of command.

If he attempted to raise his own to impose silence on these choruses of demons who tormented him, it was only with painful efforts that he could succeed in articulating some confused syllables.

He no longer talked, but he still sang; he sang the monotonous and mournful airs of his psalms, the words of which he had totally forgotten. His memory by degrees became extinct. Sometimes even, he lost the sentiment of his identity; then, at least, his state of isolation, and the memory of his misfortunes ceased to weigh upon him.

He nevertheless remembered, that about this time, having approached Swordfish Beach, attracted by an unusual noise there, he had seen it covered with soldiers and sailors, doubtless Spaniards. The idea of finding himself among men, had suddenly made his heart beat; but when he descended the declivity of the hills in order to join them, several shots were fired; the balls whistled about his ears, and, filled with terror, he had fled.

Once more hc had found himself there, but without intending it, for then he could no longer find his way, by the points of the compass, through the woods and valleys leading to the shore. Ah! how had his ancient abode changed its aspect! How many years had rolled away since he lived there! The little gravelled paths, which conducted to the grotto and the mimosa, were effaced; the mimosa, its principal branches broken, seemed buried beneath its own ruins; of his fish-pond, his bed of water-cresses, not a vestige remained; his grotto, veiled, hid beneath the thick curtains of vines and heliotropes, was no longer visible; his cabin had ceased to exist,—overthrown, swept away doubtless, by a hurricane, as his inclosure had been. He could discover the spot only by the five myrtles, which, disembarrassed of their roof of reeds and their plaster walls, had resumed their natural decorations, green and glossy, as if the hatchet had never touched them. At their feet tufts of briers and other underbrush had grown up, as formerly. The two streams, the *Linnet* and the *Stammerer*, alone had suffered no change. The one with its gentle murmur, the other with its silvery cascades, after having embraced the lawn, still continued to flow towards the sea, where they seemed to have buried, with their waves, the memory of all that had passed on their borders.

At sight of his shore, which seemed to have retained no vestige of himself, Selkirk remained a few moments, mournful and lost in his incoherent thoughts, in the midst of which this was most prominent:—Yet alive, already forgotten by the world, I have seen my traces disappear, even from this island which I have so long inhabited!

A rustling was heard in the foliage; he raised his eyes, expecting to see Marimonda swinging on the branch of a tree. Perceiving nothing, he remembered that Marimonda reposed at the Oasis; he took the road from the mountain which led thither, but when he arrived there, when he was before her tomb, covered with tall grass, he had forgotten why he came.

One of those unaccountable fits of terror, which were now more frequent than formerly, seized him, and he precipitately descended the mountain, springing from peak to peak along the rocks.

The religious sentiment, which formerly sustained Selkirk in his trials, was not entirely extinct; but it was obscured beneath his darkened reason. His religion was only that of fear. When the sea was violently agitated, when the storm howled, he prostrated himself with clasped hands; but it was no longer God whom he implored; it was the angry ocean, the thunder. He sought to disarm the genius of evil. The lightning having one day struck, not far from him, a date-palm, he worshipped the tree. His perverted faith had at last terminated in idolatry.

This was, in substance, what Alexander Selkirk related to William Dampier; what solitude had done for this man, still so young, and formerly so intelligent; this was what had become of the despiser of men, when left to his own reason.

Dampier listened with the most profound attention, interrupting him in his narrative only by exclamations of interest or of pity. When he ceased to speak, holding out his hand to him, he said:

'My boy, the lesson is a rude one, but let it be profitable to you; let it teach you that *ennui* on board a vessel, even with a Stradling, is better than *ennui* in a desert. Undoubtedly there are among us troublesome, wicked people, but fewer wicked than crack-brained. Believe, then, in friendship, especially in mine; from this day it is yours, on the faith of William Dampier.'

And he opened his arms to the young man, who threw himself into them.

On their return to the vessel, Dampier presented to Selkirk his own Bible. The latter seized it with avidity, and, after having turned over its leaves as if to find a text which presented itself to his mind, read aloud the following passage:

‘He was driven from the sons of men; and his heart was made like the beasts, and his dwelling was with the wild asses; they fed him with grass like oxen, and his body was wet with the dew of heaven.’—DANIEL v. 21.

CONCLUSION.

Capt. Rogers, in his turn, learned the misfortunes of Selkirk and became attached to him; from this moment, the sailors themselves showed him great deference; he was known among them by the name of *the governor*, and this title clung to him.

To do the honors of his island, the governor one day gave to the crews of the two vessels, the spectacle of one of his former hunts. Resuming his ancient costume, he returned to the high mountains, where, before their eyes, he started a goat, and darting in pursuit of it, over a thousand cliffs, sometimes clearing frightful abysses, by means of a vine which he seized on his passage, —this method he owed to Marimonda,—he succeeded in forcing his game to the hills of the shore. Arrived there, exhausted, panting, drawing itself up like a stag at bay, the goat stopped short. Selkirk took it living on his shoulders, and presented it to Capt. Rogers. Its ear was already slit.

By way of thanks, the captain announced that he might henceforth be connected with the expedition, with his old rank of mate, which was restored to him. For this favor Selkirk was indebted to the solicitations of Dampier.

In the same vessel with Dampier, he made another three years' voyage, visited Mexico, California, and the greater part of North America; after which, still in company with Dampier, and possessor of a pretty fortune, he returned to England, where the recital of his adventures, already made public, secured him the most honorable patronage and friendship. Among his friends, may be reckoned Steele, the co-laborer, the rival of Addison, who consecrated a long chapter to him in his publication of the Tatler.

Selkirk did not fail to visit Scotland. Passing through St. Andrew, could he help experiencing anew the desire to see his old friend pretty Kitty? Once more he appeared before the bar of the Royal Salmon. This time, on meeting, Selkirk and Catherine both experienced a sentiment of painful surprise. The latter, stouter and fuller than ever, fat and red-faced, touched the extreme limit of her fourth and last youth; the solitary of Juan Fernandez, with his gray hair, his copper complexion, could scarcely recall to the respectable hostess of the tavern the elegant pilot of the royal navy, still less the pale and blond student, of whom she had been, eighteen years before, the first and only love.

'Is it indeed you, my poor Sandy,' said she, with an accent of pity; 'I thought you were dead.'

'I have been nearly so, indeed, and a long time ago, Kitty. But who has told you of me?'

'Alas! It was my husband himself.'

'You are married then, Catherine. So much the better.'

'So much the worse rather, my friend; for, would you believe it, the old monster, bent double as he is with age and rheumatism, was bright enough to dupe me finely; to dupe me twice. In the first place, by making me believe you were dead when you were not. But he well knew, the cheat, that if I refused him once, it was because my views were turned in your direction.'

Selkirk made a movement which escaped Catherine; she continued:

'His second deception was to arrive here in triumph, in the midst of the cries of joy and embraces of the *Sea-Dogs* and *Old Pilots*. One would have thought he had in his pockets all the mines of Guinea and Peru. He did not say so, but I thought it could not be otherwise; and I married him, since I believed you no longer living. His trick having succeeded, he then told me of his shipwreck, his complete ruin. Ah! with what a good heart would I have sent him packing! But it was too late, and it became necessary that the Royal Salmon, founded by the honorable Andrew Felton, should furnish subsistence for two; and this is the reason why, Mr. Selkirk, you find me still here, a prisoner in my bar, and cursing all the captains who make the tour of the world only to come afterwards and impose upon poor and inexperienced young girls!'

Selkirk had not at first understood the lamentations of Catherine; but a twilight commenced to dawn in his ideas; he divined that his name had been used for an act of baseness; and, without being able to account for it, he felt the return of an old leaven of spite, an old hatred revived.

'Who is your husband? What is his name?' asked he, in a loud voice and with a tone of authority.

'Do not grow angry, Sandy? Do not seek a quarrel with him now. What is done, is done; I am his wife, do you understand? It is of no use to recall the past.'

'And who thinks of recalling it? I simply asked you who he was?'

'You will be prudent; you promise me? Well! do you see him yonder, in the second stall, at the same place he formerly occupied? He has just poured out some gin to those sailors, and is drinking with them. It is he who is standing up with an apron on.'

'Stradling!' exclaimed Selkirk, with sparkling eyes. But at the sight of this apron, finding his old captain become a waiter, his hatred and projects of vengeance were suddenly extinguished.

Alexander Selkirk returned to England in 1712. The history of his captivity in the Island of Juan Fernandez had appeared in the papers; several apocryphal relations had been already published, when in 1717, Daniel De Foe published his *Robinson Crusoe.*

He is really the same personage; but in this latter version, the Island of Juan Fernandez, in spite of distance and geographical impossibilities, is peopled with savage Caribs; Marimonda is transformed into the simple Friday; history is turned into romance, but this romance is elevated to all the dignity of a philosophical treatise.

Rendering full justice to the merit of the writer, we must nevertheless acknowledge that he has completely altered, in a mental view, the physiognomy of his model. Robinson is not a man suffering entire isolation; he has a companion, and the savages are incessantly making inroads around him. It is the European developing the resources of his industry, to contend at once with an unproductive land and the dangers created by his enemies.

Selkirk has no enemies to repulse, and he inhabits a fruitful country. He needs, before every thing else, the presence of man, one of those fraternal affections in which he refuses to believe. His sufferings originate in his very solitude. In solitude, Robinson improves and perfects himself; Selkirk, at first as full of resources as he, ends by becoming discouraged andbrutified.

Which of the two is most true to nature?

The first is an ideal being, for in no quarter of the globe has there ever been found one analogous to the Robinson of De Foe; the other, on the contrary, is to be met with every where, denying the dependence of an isolated individual; but this dependence, even in the midst of a prodigal nature, if it is not to the honor of man, is to the honor of society at large.

Notwithstanding all that has been said, the solitary is a man imbruted, vegetating, deprived of his crown. 'Solitude is sweet only in the vicinity of great cities.'[1] By an admirable decree of Providence, the isolated being is an imperfect being; man is completed by man.

[1]

Bernardin de St. Pierre. Seneca had said: *Miscenda et alternanda sunt solitudo et frequentia.*

Notwithstanding the false maxims of a deceitful philosophy, it is to the social state that we owe, from the greatest to the least, the courage which animates and sustains us; God has created us to live there and to love one another; it is for this reason that selfishness is a shameful vice, a crime! It is, so to speak, an infringement of one of the great laws of Nature.

THE END.

www.ingramcontent.com/pod-product-compliance
Lightning Source LLC
Chambersburg PA
CBHW060801310726
48980CB00002B/184

* 9 7 8 3 7 3 2 6 2 1 0 2 6 *